TWO GUNS NORTH

Jason Brand's latest assignment takes him into the mountains, searching for two missing men — a Deputy US Marshal and a government geologist. But this apparently routine assignment turns out to be anything but. For Bodie the Stalker, hunting a brutal killer, rides the same trail. It's just another manhunt for him — until he finds himself on the wrong end of the chase. But then Bodie meets Brand. And when they join forces, it's as if Hell itself has come to the high country . . .

NEIL HUNTER

BODIE MEETS BRAND:
TWO GUNS NORTH

Complete and Unabridged

LINFORD
Leicester

First published in Great Britain in 2015

First Linford Edition
published 2016

A catalogue record for this book is available
from the British Library.

ISBN 978–1–4448–3079–8

Published by
F. A. Thorpe (Publishing)
Anstey, Leicestershire

Set by Words & Graphics Ltd.
Anstey, Leicestershire
Printed and bound in Great Britain by
T. J. International Ltd., Padstow, Cornwall

This book is printed on acid-free paper

1

'*Hai!*'

The triumphant cry rang out loud and clear. It was followed by the sound of a human form striking the padded mat covering the floor of the gymnasium.

'You are improving,' the Japanese instructor, Kito, said. 'Today you fall down like expert!'

Jason Brand glared up at the impassive face of the Japanese from his position on the mat. If there was one thing he couldn't stand it was Kito's sense of humor. It was most definitely weird.

'All for today,' Kito pronounced sharply.

Brand climbed to his feet and faced the instructor across the mat, returning Kito's ceremonial bow.

'Today you are good,' Kito said

seriously, and coming from him it was praise indeed. 'Always must practice.'

Brand nodded. He turned and left the gymnasium, making his way to the changing room. He'd known the moment he had stepped on the mat that he was fully fit again. The long weeks of training, the punishing exercise each and every day, had burned away the lethargy that had settled over him on his return to Washington. The affair in Montana, and the shock of his returning memory, had finally caught up with him. Plus the wounding he had received at the hands of Jerome Cortland during their final confrontation. His body had simply rebelled and it had taken long weeks for Brand to recover. With Virginia Maitland back in New York, with a possible trip back to London in order to finalize the affairs of the company she had inherited and almost lost, Brand was not going to see much of her in the next months. She had put off dealing with her business until Brand had recovered enough for her to leave.

Now he was feeling better. Stronger — impatient even — and ready for a new assignment, though to himself only would he admit to succumbing to moments of doubt. When he felt the dull, nagging headaches that returned sporadically. They were not as bad as they had been and he was able to function normally. He kept the information to himself, not wanting to give any suggestions he still suffered from them. If he had mentioned the headaches to the department doctor he might have been pulled back out of service. Brand didn't want that. He wanted — needed — to be back on the job. So he put up with the discomfort. Concealed it and kept it to himself.

He was sure McCord had something for him. The summons to his office had been short and sweet, and Brand was sure he knew what that meant. The thought excited him. It would good to be back in the field. Cooped up as he had been for the last long weeks Brand felt like a wild pony that had been penned in, deprived of its natural habitat. Now he sensed the gate being opened and he was ready to be off.

He had a quick wash, dried and dressed, then made his way up from the gym. Bright sunlight glanced in through the windows as he made his way along the empty corridor to McCord's office. He knocked sharply on the door and went in.

McCord was leaning back in his seat, gazing out of his window, and looking almost benevolent. Almost. Brand sat down and stretched his long legs, studying his boots and decided it was time he bought some new ones.

'Feeling fit enough to take on the world, are we?' McCord asked without moving from his comfortable position.

'A small part of it maybe,' Brand answered.

McCord grunted and straightened up, swiveling his chair around to face Brand across his desk. He opened a folder on his desk, peering at the contents as if he had never seen them before. He cleared his throat.

'Two months ago a government geologist, Joseph Calvin, making a field study in the San Juan range, simply vanished. His reports stopped coming back to Washington. He failed to keep in contact with his family, which for him was completely out of character. When his disappearance became too obvious to ignore any longer an attempt was made to locate him. A Deputy US Marshal in the New Mexico area at the time was assigned to look into the matter. Name of Hec Rankin. He also disappeared. A geologist failing to maintain contact is one thing. The disappearance of a professional lawman is too much of a coincidence.'

Brand stood up and crossed to the large map pinned to the wall. He circled an area with his finger. 'It's a hell of a big area. And high mountain country, too. You could lose an army in there and never find it.'

'I'm sure you'll find a way to locate those missing men,' McCord said. 'There could be a simple explanation to the whole thing. On the other hand it might be more involved. But we have been requested to look into it, so we do just that.'

'When do I leave?'

'Travel arrangements have all been taken care off. When you reach Santa Fe you'll find a horse ready for you to pick up. All the details are in the file.' McCord slid the folder across the desk for Brand to pick up. 'I'm beginning to think I make life too easy for you people. Perhaps it's time I stopped looking after you so much. This assignment is one my maiden Aunt could take on.'

Brand was still grinning long after he had left McCord's office. He took a stroll down to the firing range that was located in the cellars beneath the main building. Here he spent some time with the armorer, Whitehead. The stocky, gray-haired man knew more about guns and their uses than any man Brand had known. He looked after the weapons of all McCord's operatives.

'I hear you're off in the morning,' Whitehead said as Brand appeared in the door of his workshop.

'Everything ready?'

Whitehead nodded briskly. 'Both handguns and your rifle.' He reached across his bench and selected the weapons from the selection on display.

Brand took his .45 caliber Colt Peacemaker, fingers curling around the slightly grained wood grips. The raised grain allowed him a better grip on the wood. The moment he picked it up the gun became an extension of his hand. It was familiar, comfortable in his grasp. He tried the action and found it smooth, the trigger dropping the hammer at the slightest increase of pressure from his finger. Now Whitehead passed across the Colt special. It had started out as a standard .45 caliber Colt. Whitehead had adapted it by cutting down the barrel to two inches, requiring the removal of the ejector sleeve and rod. The foresection of the trigger guard had also been cut away, allowing easy access to the trigger itself. The butt grips had also been shaved down and shaped to fit Brand's hand. Brand had used the weapon on a number of occasions, and despite its limitations it had proved to be an effective, close-quarter weapon. It was a strictly experimental adaptation Whitehead had created for Brand, more for the armorer's pleasure than anything. Brand had used one previously and since he had been deprived of the weapon Whitehead had built him another.

'Try not to lose this one,' Whitehead said.

'Do my best.'

Brand took the guns, and additional boxes of cartridges. He made his way to the firing range and spent a half hour shooting at paper targets. His ears rang from the echoing blast of the shots that were magnified by the confining walls of the cellar.

'Satisfactory?' Whitehead asked when Brand returned to the workshop.

'Yeah,' Brand said.

He collected his rifle, more ammunition, and made his way back outside. Returning to his room he began to pack for his trip.

$$\star \quad \star \quad \star$$

Fine rain was drifting out of a gray sky as Brand's train pulled out of the Washington depot. After a final conference with McCord he had had left for the depot early, eating breakfast at a small restaurant nearby. Now, as the train chugged and clanked its way from the city, Brand settled back in his seat. The prospect of the long journey ahead did little to raise his spirits.

He stared the length of the Pullman car. It was empty save for a middle-aged, prosperous-looking couple down at the far end. Brand stirred restlessly.

There was nothing else for it. He was just going to have to put up with his own company.

The door at the far end of the car opened and the Conductor came through. He spoke briefly to the couple, then made his way along the swaying car to where Brand sat.

'Mister Brand?'

'Yeah.'

The Conductor scratched his chin. 'I, er, got a young feller back there wants to talk to you. Says it's important.'

'So?'

'See, he's from third class. Company regulations and all ... well, he ain't supposed to even set foot inside a Pullman car.'

'He give you a name?' Brand asked. Glancing past the Conductor he could see a vague, featureless figure standing on the opposite side of the glass-topped compartment door. 'Say why he wants to see me?'

The Conductor shook his head. 'No, sir. He won't tell me a thing 'cept he

10

has to see you. I got the feeling he's pretty serious about it, though.'

Brand took out his wallet and slid out a ten-dollar bill. He folded it and pressed it into the Conductor's willing palm.

'Those regulations. I figure we can bend 'em a little?'

The Conductor smiled. 'Sure. I guess so.'

Brand watched him walk back down to the end of the car and open the door. He said something to the waiting figure, then stepped aside and let him through. The young man who entered the car hesitated for a moment, eyes roving back and forth. Then he moved along the car, long legs carrying him quickly to stand in front of Brand.

He was close on eighteen, his tanned face yet to see its first growth of whiskers. He was holding his battered hat in his hands. A thick mass of dark hair, shaggy around the collar of his worn short coat, fell low across his forehead. His mouth was firm, held in a taut line that might have indicated barely contained anger. But it was the eyes that attracted Brand's attention more than anything. They were a sharp, piercing shade of blue. The boy was staring through them at Brand as if he was looking deep into his very soul. Something in the earnest expression unsettled and intrigued Brand.

'Conductor said you wanted to talk to me.'

The boy nodded. 'Yes, sir.'

His accent was foreign to this part of the country. It placed him from the Southwest. New Mexico maybe. Or even somewhere in West Texas.

Brand smiled at the boy's monosyllabic reply.

'You got the better of me, boy. You know who I am, but you didn't give a name to the Conductor. Be easier if I knew who you are.'

'Well, ma called me Adam,' the boy said. 'So I guess that makes my full name Adam Brand. *I'm your son!*'

2

Smoke from the locomotive whipped by the rain-streaked window. The wheels had settled into a steady rattle. A rhythmic, repetitive sound. The Pullman car swayed gently as the train took a curve, soft green hills seeming to swell up on either side as the tracks cut through a wide embankment.

Staring up at the boy Jason Brand flicked a hand in the direction of the seat facing him. He watched the boy sit down, aware of a familiarity in the young face, and realized with a shock he was looking at himself. Or how he had looked eighteen years ago.

'Eighteen-seventy,' the boy said. 'The Comanch' took you captive after they killed your family. They took you to a camp on the Llano. Quanah Parker was there. The Comanche who led the raid had already taken your sister there. His name was Three Finger. He . . . he murdered your sister before you could get her away. But you escaped with a girl you met in the camp. Another captive. Lisa Hoyle . . . '

The years slipped away, layers of his mind peeling back, letting the memories of that time return. Brand had no difficulty in recalling the events, the places, the people . . .

. . . *the girl had brought him food, kneeling before him in the dust of Three Finger's camp. She was young, his own age, and she was naked, her lithe, long-limbed body firmly developed. Her cropped hair was fair under the matted dirt, her eyes a startling shade of blue . . .*

'*I don't even know your name,*' *she had said later.*

'*Jason Brand.*'

'*I'm Lisa Hoyle.*'

She had been with him when he had made his break from the camp. Too late to save his sister, Liz, from the Comanche called Three Finger. Yet they

14

had survived. Fighting the land and the relentless pursuit of the savage Three Finger, their desperate situation drawing them close. Brand had killed the Comanche . . . but more violence had reared its head when they had reached the refuge of a dirty border town and a trio of local hardcases had tried to take Lisa from Brand. He had been pushed into using the violent skills that were to become almost a curse throughout his life.

In that little town without a name, in a small room, the closeness that had grown during their long flight from captivity spilled over into a physical need. They had made love with the urgent passion of the young, tasting new sensations, seeking more of the same until there had been no more to give, nothing more to be taken. Yet even that time had ended in bitterness, a rift growing between them because of Brand's burning desire for vengeance against the men who had deserted his family in their time of need, and Lisa's reluctance to accept his violent ways.

'*Surely you can go to the law? Or the Army? Can't you?*' she asked.

'*And what would they do? Stick up a few posters. Hell, Lisa, I could get to be an old man waiting for something to happen.*'

'*You could get to be a very dead young man the way you're acting.*'

'*My folks are dead. If those three bastards had stuck with us I might still have family. I don't figure to forget that. I won't forget even when those three are dead and buried.*'

'*I think you're wrong, Jason, terribly wrong. All you're doing is living on bitterness. On hatred. It's no way to exist.*'

'*I don't reckon I have to listen to you. Ain't nobody's business but mine what I do with my life. You should of left it alone, Lisa. Now it's between us.*'

And it had remained between them up until the time Brand left Lisa with relatives in El Paso. Brand had exorcised her from his life, moving on, and as the years passed she had become little more than a memory.

'And she wouldn't let anyone in the family tell you about me,' the boy was saying.

Brand dragged himself back to the present, aware of the boy, Adam's, intense stare.

'Did she still hate me that much?' he asked.

Adam shook his dark head. 'I don't think she ever hated you at all. It was what she saw in you that scared her. All she ever wanted was peace and quiet. She used to say you were so full of revenge and violence. She'd seen too much of that herself.'

Brand didn't need to question that. He recalled how Lisa had made her feelings known on the matter.

'Where is she now?' he asked.

The boy was silent for a moment, staring out at the green countryside blurring past the window.

'She died eight months back. She'd been ill for a couple of years on and off.

Some kind of lung disease the doctor said. They did what they could but . . . '

'I wish she'd got in touch,' Brand said. 'I would have come to see you both.' The moment he uttered the words Brand felt like a fraud. He realized how false they sounded. 'Hell, boy, you got to give me a chance to take it in. Isn't every day a man comes face to face with a son he never knew he had. Especially when he's near enough full grown as well.'

'I was going to write,' Adam said. 'Then I figured there was a better way.' He paused, adding, 'Anyhow I wanted to meet you.'

'What about Lisa's kin?'

'Aunt Laura died five years back. Uncle Ben still has the store. He had to take on a feller to run it when I said I didn't want to work behind a counter.'

'Didn't he want you to stay?'

'He knew I was restless. I told him how I felt about looking for you and he said it was time I did something about it.' Adam gave an embarrassed smile. 'So here I am.'

'How long you been looking?'

'Close on four months. You move around a lot. And you keep vanishing.'

It was Brand's turn to smile. 'It's something my job makes me do.'

'That's what Colonel Mundy told me.'

'Alex Mundy?'

Adam nodded. 'I met him a few weeks back. When I told him who I was he said he'd help. He told me the work you do means you have to stay in the shadows, and he made me promise not to say anything about what he told me.'

'Seems I owe Alex a favor.'

'He told me you'd say that too. Said to tell you to forget it.'

An awkwardness fell between them. The silence stretched as they both sought the right words. The strain was broken by the appearance of a Negro attendant from the dining car.

'We serve lunch at noon, sir,' he told

Brand. 'Would you like to reserve a table?'

Brand nodded. 'For two. Will you ask the Conductor to come forward?'

The Negro nodded and left them.

'You got any luggage?' Brand asked.

Adam said, 'Back down the train.'

'Go and fetch it.'

'Yes, sir,' Adam said and stood up.

Brand watched him go, letting out a relieved sigh.

Judas Priest, he thought, *I'm getting too old for surprises like this.*

The Conductor appeared. 'Mister Brand?'

'Can you make out a ticket for the boy? He's going to join me up here.'

'All the way to Santa Fe?'

Brand took his wallet out again. 'Yeah, all the way.' Brand grinned suddenly. 'We've a lot of talking to do. Looks like we'll need every minute of this damn trip to do it.'

The Conductor glanced up from writing out the ticket, frowning at the grinning man. He made no comment.

20

It wasn't his job to try and figure out what the passengers were talking about. And he had been in the job too long to be surprised at anything they said, or did.

Adam returned carrying a pair of saddlebags over one shoulder and a bedroll under his arm. He had a Winchester rifle in one hand. Brand helped him stow his stuff away.

'That loaded?' Brand asked.

Adam held up the rifle. 'Yes, sir, but the breech is empty.'

Brand held out a hand and took the weapon, examining it. 'Can you use it?'

'I hit what I aim at,' Adam said with the confidence of youth. Then he quickly added, 'Mind I've only ever shot at targets or game.'

Brand put the rifle down. 'Well don't sound so glum about it. Ain't a rule you have to go shoot at a man just so's you can say you done it.'

Adam flushed with anger. 'I didn't mean that,' he said sharply.

'I wasn't saying you did, boy. Hell,

don't mind me. I'm just taking a little longer than usual getting used to being a father.'

A laugh rose in Adam's throat.

'I say something funny?'

'No. Just something I'm trying to figure out.'

'*What?*'

'Do I call you father? Or pa? Or what?'

'Looks like we got problems already. Why don't we leave it open? You decide what feels right.'

'Alright,' Adam said. He leaned back in his seat. 'This is nice. Lot better than back there. They always let you travel like this?'

'No. It's just that sometimes they like to coat the pill with sugar so you don't think you have it so bad when the hard times come.'

'Where you heading now?'

'Santa Fe first. Then up into the San Juan Mountains.'

'You after somebody?'

'Looking for somebody. Two men in fact. Seems they got themselves lost up in the mountains.'

'Can I ride with you?' Adam asked, eagerness shining in his eyes.

'No. But you can wait for me in Santa Fe.'

Adam's shoulders sagged. 'What am I going to do there? I don't see why I can't come with you.'

'I'm not about to argue over this, boy. No way of knowing what I'll find when I take to those mountains. I won't have time to look out for you.'

'I'm not a kid,' Adam retorted. 'I can look after myself.'

'Listen to me, Adam, and remember. Most of the time the job I do is dirty and downright unhealthy. A lot of the people I get mixed up with are the kind who would rather kill you than talk. I have a gun in my hand a lot of the time because it's the only sure way to stay alive. I've had to kill a lot of men, and it isn't something I'm proud of. But it's the life I lead. Give yourself a few more years and you'll see there are some mean folk walking around. Don't fool yourself into thinking that just 'cause you've blown holes in a few tin cans it makes you eligible for my kind of business. It doesn't, boy.'

'I'm sorry,' Adam said. 'I got no right to push myself on you. Maybe it was the wrong thing to do.'

'You can quit that talk,' Brand said. 'Look, we're going to be stuck on this train for a few days. Plenty of time to talk things out. No need to rush.'

Adam nodded. 'I guess so.' He began to relax, gazing out the window again. Abruptly he looked back at Brand. 'Is it true you were a US Marshal? Tell me about it.'

Brand realized something there and then. This train ride certainly wasn't going to be boring. He wasn't going to be allowed to get bored. In fact it looked as if he was going to be filling every minute. Just as he had said to the Conductor. He had all those lost years to make up for and the way it was shaping up, he wasn't going to be allowed to miss out a single day.

24

3

They arrived in Santa Fe almost six hours behind schedule. A freight train had suffered one of its boxcars jumping the tracks at Raton Pass and the repair crews had a difficult time getting it back on the rails. Eventually the track was cleared and the delayed train rolled on. It was almost midnight when it arrived at the Santa Fe depot.

'I don't know about you, but all I want is a bed to fall into,' Brand said as they made their way up the street.

'Sounds good to me.'

They reached the sprawling bulk of Santa Fe's largest and most celebrated hotel, La Fonda. Brand led the way inside, crossing the dim, lamp-lit lobby. A sleepy figure stirred in the shadows behind the desk.

'*Buenos noches, señor,*' the Mexican said.

'Hello, Emilio.'

The round-faced Mexican leaned forward, smiling when he recognized Brand.

'*Señor* Brand. Welcome back to La Fonda. It has been too long. Are you well?'

'Fine. Emilio, do you have a nice cool room. With a pair of soft beds?'

'For you, *Señor* Brand, always.' Emilio picked up a key. 'How long will you be with us this time?'

'I'll be riding out in the morning. I have some business. Might be gone a while. But my boy, here, will be staying on until I get back. See he has everything he needs, Emilio. I'll settle up when I get back.'

'But of course.' Emilio glanced over Brand's shoulder at Adam who was in the shadows on the far side of the lobby. '*Señor*, did I hear you say . . . '

'The boy is my son, Emilio.'

'Then he is doubly welcome. Though I did not realize you had a son, *Señor* Brand. He looks a fine boy.'

'Yeah,' Brand found himself saying, with a feeling he could only describe as pride. 'Oh, hell, Emilio, I only found out about him myself a few days back.'

Emilio's smile broadened. '*Si*. I understand.'

'You can wipe that smirk off your face, you old devil. When I get back maybe I'll tell you all about it.'

'*Bueno*! Then do not worry. Emilio will take good care of him while you are away.' He handed Brand the key. 'Sleep well, my friend.'

Brand checked the room number, then led the way up the shadowed stairs and along the cool passage. He unlocked the door of the room and dumped his gear on the floor, moving to light the lamp set on a round table.

'Get yourself sorted out,' he told Adam. 'I'll be back in a while.'

'Where are you going?'

Brand opened his bag and took out his gun belt. He strapped it on, checking that the Colt was fully loaded. 'I'm going over to the Federal Building.

I need to check if any messages came in for me.'

Adam took off his coat, yawning. 'All right,' he said.

'You want anything bringing back?'

'No.'

The night air was cool. Brand left the hotel and strode across the nearly deserted plaza, skirting the monument erected to commemorate the dead of the battle of Valverde. The Federal Building stood on Palace Avenue and this too looked deserted. Brand went inside, his boots echoing on the hard floor. He saw there was a light showing in the town Marshal's office. The Marshal himself, hunched over a sheaf of papers, glanced up as Brand entered.

'I help you, mister?'

'Name's Brand. You might have some messages for me?'

The Marshal leaned back in his chair. He was a stocky, stern-faced man in his early forties, dark hair starting to go gray.

'Nate Dembrow. Been expecting

28

you,' he said. 'Not this late though got to say.'

'Freight train came off the rails at Raton Pass. Held us up some.'

'Well nothing come through for you,' the Marshal said. 'Washington was on to me a few days back. Asked if I'd cooperate with you.'

'Be grateful for anything you can tell me, Marshal.'

'Sit down, Mister Brand. Coffee?'

'Thanks.'

As he poured a couple of mugs of coffee Dembrow said, 'Not much more I can tell you that you probably already heard. This geologist feller — Joseph Calvin — he dropped in to see me 'fore he lit out for the San Juans. Seemed a sensible kind of feller. Way he talked it seemed he'd done this kind of thing before. Didn't seem the kind likely to get himself lost up a mountain.'

Brand took the mug of coffee. 'He give you any idea the area he was heading for?'

The Marshal crossed to a map of the

territory pinned to the wall behind his desk.

'Said he'd be covering a pretty wide area. Looking for mineral deposits. Aimed to travel north. Maybe a little northwest. Figuring on forty, fifty, miles in. High country.'

Dembrow ringed the area on the map with his finger.

'Anything up that way?' Brand asked.

The Marshal shrugged. 'All I know is it's pretty wild country. Hell of large area. Never been that far in myself. Nigh on uninhabited far as I know. Did once hear of a settlement up there. Keep themselves to themselves. No bother to anyone. Truth be told there ain't anyone else up there to bother.'

'What about the other feller who went looking for Calvin?'

'Hec Rankin? Same goes for him. Deputy US Marshal. No man's fool. Known him for nigh on four years. Dependable man. No damn greenhorn.'

Brand drained his coffee mug and

placed it on the desk.

'If that's so, what the hell happened to 'em?'

Dembrow shrugged. 'Like I said, you know as much as I do, Mister Brand.'

Brand stood up. 'I'll be heading out in the morning. Anything occurs to me I'll drop by.'

The Marshal followed him to the door. 'Sorry I couldn't be more help. Fact is there ain't much to tell. Calvin was here and rode out. He didn't come back. Hec Rankin went to look for him and now they both ain't come back.'

'Be seeing you, Marshal.'

He made his way back to La Fonda. Santa Fe had gained a degree of late nightlife since he had been inside the Marshal's office. Brand heard music. From a shadowed alley came the muffled protests of an excited woman. The words were in Spanish, and even if Brand hadn't understood the language he could have deciphered the meaning of the not too insistent protest. As he moved on the sounds trailed away into a healthy sigh of contentment.

Reaching the hotel Brand made his way up to the room. He let himself in and found it in darkness. From Adam's bed came the sound of deep, steady breathing. Brand undressed and eased into his own bed. No point disturbing the boy, he decided.

★ ★ ★

Adam was still sleeping when Brand got up with the first rays of the sun. Crossing to the washstand he tipped water from the jug into a wide bowl and sluiced his face. Grabbing a towel Brand dried himself, looking out through the window.

Far to the northwest he could make out the shimmering peaks of the San Juan range rising soft and mist-shrouded through the early haze. Somewhere in those distant heights were two lost men. Men he had to find. He hoped they would still be alive. For all he knew they could already be dead.

Buried in solitary graves, away from prying eyes.

Judas Priest, he thought, *you're starting to get morbid.*

Brand pulled on dark pants and a gray shirt. His suit was hung out of the way in the wardrobe. He strapped on the Colt, checking the revolver was loaded and his belt loops full. He did the same to his rifle. The adapted revolver sat snug in the shoulder holster. He covered it with a shortcoat. When he turned from the window he saw Adam sitting up in bed, watching him.

'I figured you were set for the day,' Brand said. He tossed the towel to the boy. 'Splash some of that water on your face. It'll wake you up proper.'

Adam threw back the covers, easing his lean shape off the bed. 'I am awake,' he muttered.

Brand sensed Adam's sullen mood and knew what had prompted it.

'Boy, you can sulk all damn day if you've a mind to. Won't change a thing.

You ain't coming with me.'

Adam bent over the basin and sluiced water on his face.

'So what am I supposed to do around here while you're gone?'

'You'll think of something. If you need for anything go talk to Emilio. He's a good friend. He's promised to keep an eye on you.'

'I ain't a baby,' Adam exploded, throwing the towel across the room. 'I don't need a damn nursemaid.'

'You could sure do with a lesson in manners, boy. Now just quit fooling around and feeling sorry for yourself. Give me time to get this job done then we can have ourselves a chance at working out what we're going to do.'

Brand tugged on his boots, stamping his feet down into the snug leather. He recalled Adam's outburst, a wry smile on his lips. The boy had done exactly what Brand himself would have done at the same age. Watching him Brand found himself imagining he was staring into a mirror. It was a reflection that was half a lifetime old. So many of Adam's mannerisms were Brand's own. It was like having a living shadow following him around. Part of him, yet separate. It pleased him — and it also scared the hell out of him.

They went down and ate breakfast in silence. Adam had retreated into a shell that excluded even his father. Brand left him to it. It was only when they were approaching the livery stable where Brand's rented horse was waiting for him that Adam broke his silence.

'I guess I'm sorry,' he said awkwardly.

Brand smiled. 'Never liked having to apologize myself.'

They went inside the stable where Brand was shown his horse. It was a strong-looking chestnut with a white streak in its mane. The animal had some spirit, which Brand liked. Give him a mount with a good character. The chestnut had a good build. It would need that for the hilly terrain they would be negotiating. He began to saddle up.

'How long will you be away?'

'Hard to tell. Few days. No way of knowing until I get down to it.'

He finished saddling up and tied on his gear, pushed his rifle into the boot. He had two large filled canteens of water to add. Adam fell in beside him as they as they walked outside. Brand took out his wallet and slid out some money. He handed it to Adam.

'If you need anything else just ask Emilio.'

'Thanks,' Adam said. He watched Brand mount up and gather his reins. 'You take care now.'

Brand nodded. 'Be back as soon as I can. See you then, boy.'

'I'll be here,' Adam said. He raised a hand in a quick gesture as Brand moved off. 'I'll be waiting — *pa*.'

4

For the second time in as many days Bodie had lost the trail. It annoyed the hell out of him when that happened. It wasn't as if he was some damned greenhorn. He'd been tracking men for more years than he cared to recall and it purely didn't seem natural for him to keep missing Monk's trail.

Thaddeus Monk was wanted in a number of territories. His list of crimes included robbery and assault. He was also a multiple killer, having willfully shot down a number of men and latterly a woman. Monk had no redeeming qualities. He held laws and social graces in contempt, happy to go about his brutal ways with total disregard for the world around him. He was also a hard man to catch, which was why Bodie had been asked to go after him.

A collective of concerned business-men had hired him, aware of Bodie's reputation and his tracking skills. They also understood the way Bodie worked. He didn't play by the rules. Borders meant nothing to the man. Once he took on a contract he would follow his man to the very gates of Hell and snatch him from the hands of the Devil himself. The incentive here, apart from the need to get Monk taken down, was the added financial bonus Bodie would get on top of the official bounties pinned to Monk.

People might not have liked Bodie but they sure as hell couldn't do without him. He had no equals in the bounty business. Put Bodie on a wanted man's trail and the matter was settled even before the fugitive was in his sights.

It was close on noon. Hot and dusty. The sky wasn't showing a scrap of cloud, so when Bodie saw the stream coming down off the slope close by he decided it was time to rest up. He eased out of the saddle, stretching his back to loosen the nagging ache and led his horse to the water. The big gray swung its head and he could swear it scowled at him as if to say not before time.

'Go drink, hoss,' he said. 'Ain't much fun for me either.

The horse snorted and wandered to the stream to drink. Bodie unhitched his big canteen and tipped out what was left of the warm water. He knelt upstream from where the horse was drinking and rinsed out the canteen before he refilled it. Bodie dropped his hat on the ground and dunked his head into the water. Took away the sweat and dust. He threw back his head, his shaggy hair spraying water in all directions. He felt only a little better for that but at least it cleared his head and cooled him a mite.

He loosened the saddle and slid it off, using the blanket to wipe down the gray's back. The animal continued to drink until Bodie pulled it away from the stream and found it a patch of reasonable grass for it to feed.

'Fool horse. You'd drink that stream dry if I didn't stop you.'

He figured he was entitled to a break, so he built a fire to heat water for coffee. It took him some time to find suitable dry wood but a half-hour later he was able to smell the aroma of coffee bubbling in the blackened pot over the flames. He decided not to cook a meal and made do with a couple of thick slices of jerked beef. It was pretty damn tasteless and made his jaw ache from chewing, but the strong coffee made up for that.

Bodie sat with his back pressed against a slab of hot rock and watched a scaly lizard sunning itself a few yards away from him.

'Hell of a life you got there, son,' he said. 'Just laze all damn day in the sun, flicking your tongue out ever' time an insect gets close. Enough to make a man jealous.'

Either the lizard didn't hear him, or it was ignoring him. It lay motionless.

Didn't even turn its head when he spoke.

'Well the hell with you,' Bodie said.

Then he decided he needed some human company to make up for the fact he was sitting there talking to a damn lizard.

He finished his pot of coffee, doused the fire and rinsed out his pot and tin mug. He saddled up, then stowed his gear in his possibles sack and tied it on over the saddlebags. He checked his horse, looking for anything that might have stuck in the animal's hooves. He inspected for cuts on the gray's legs. A missed graze could easily become infected during a long ride through rough country. When he was done he swung into the saddle and turned in the direction of Monk's faint tracks.

He hadn't missed the way they were angling in the direction of the distant mountains. Bodie raised his eyes to take in the peaks. The San Juan range covered the horizon. A lot of mountains. Plenty of places for someone like

Monk to hide himself away. Bodie had been hoping Monk might avoid the range. It seemed he had been wrong. It didn't make his job impossible — just harder once a man worked his way into those foothills and high slopes. A thousand places to hide. To disappear.

Bodie kept the mountains in his sight as he rode. Something at the back of his mind was making itself known. He didn't press the thought. Simply let it come until it was fully formed.

'Monk, you just made life easier for me.'

Bodie had recalled something he'd heard way back. A mention of Monk having family way back in the San Juan Mountains. They had an isolated outfit where they lived, not exactly welcoming visitors so the telling went. Bodie hadn't thought much about it at the time, but now he figured maybe he'd learned where Monk could be going.

Family ties were strong in some people. Thaddeus Monk might have been a mean sonofabitch, but even he had filial connections, and maybe right now he needed family around him. Bodie had seen the posters issued by various lawmen featuring Monk's likeness, and the phrase a face only a mother could love had sprung to mind. Monk was a hulking brute of a man and his thickset face did little to offset that.

Since Monk's last crime spree, where he had killed three, including a young woman during a bank holdup that had netted him over 8,000 dollars, he had been on the move. The murder of the woman had been the last nail in Monk's coffin. His previous crimes were bad enough but the wanton killing of the woman had pushed Thaddeus Monk across the line. No one, not even those in the criminal fraternity, wanted any more to do with him.

Added to Monk's atrocities and the thing that now excluded him from any redemption was the fact he had shot the woman in the back. That fact ostracized him from practically every level of society, marking him as a man alone. A pariah no one wanted to be associated with. Monk had never been a man who yearned for company. Now the few friends he might have had shunned him. He was on his own.

And that was why he was on his way into the mountains. Away from civilization. Seeking the one place where he wouldn't be judged. Into the circle of family.

Well, hell, son, Bodie decided, *that circle is about to get broken.*

He eased his way through the foothills, letting his horse choose its path. The gray was smart. It picked its way over the loose detritus that had tumbled to the base of the slopes. Bodie lounged in the saddle, scanning the way ahead. The tree-lined slopes above showed dark and green against the starker color of the earth and rocks. The timber grew in close ranks, thick and spreading out in all directions. Once Bodie reached the trees he would have better cover, but so would Monk. That was always the way. What life gave with one hand it took away with the other.

Bodie unhooked his canteen and took a swallow. The water had already started to lose the chill it had in the stream. At least it was fresh.

As he hung the canteen back in place Bodie's downcast eyes spotted faint horse tracks. He reined in the gray and swung out of the saddle, crouching over the hoof prints. They were a few hours old he judged, but they were moving in the right direction. Tugging on the reins Bodie walked his horse for a while, following the trail.

'You keep on running, Monk. Just don't look back because I'm on my way, you sonofabitch.'

The gray turned its head and stared at him. Bodie stroked its sleek neck.

'I ain't crazy, horse. Just craving someone to talk to.'

As the afternoon wore on Bodie found himself moving into the timber. Once he rode through the first spread of the forest he felt the heat slip away.

He was enclosed in the shadowed coolness of the trees, the high canopy of intertwined branches acting like a protective shield against the sun's heat. Bodie didn't mind. The oppressive heat of the sun made for uncomfortable riding. Out of the sun's direct glare he felt better.

Bodie dismounted again, leading the horse as he checked Monk's trail. The crisscross shadows from the trees and undergrowth cut down the amount of light. It would be easy to lose the trail he was following if he allowed himself to ease off. Bodie stopped often to maintain contact with the tracks. He figured he was still on line. Monk was moving in a pretty straight line. The man knew where he was going and it was plain he knew his piece of the country up here.

Maybe too damn well, Bodie decided as the sudden crash of a rifle shot broke the silence.

The .44–40 slug burned past his ear. The gray pulled away in panic and

Bodie went to ground, his breath driven from his lungs as he landed. The shot had come from his left and from behind.

A damned backshooter.

Bodie could respect a man who faced him with a gun. He considered a backshooter nothing more than a coward. And the thought made him mad.

As he dropped he cleared the heavy Colt from his holster and hugged it close as he feigned injury.

He was hoping that playing dead might draw out the shooter. It might get him a slug in the back but Bodie was figuring the man might be curious enough to want to take a look.

5

Time dragged. Bodie stayed where he was. After a time the birds that had scattered with the sound of the shot returned and settled. Bodie felt the sun warm on his back. The smell of the loamy forest floor was strong in his nostrils. His senses told him whoever had driven that shot at him was still around. Most likely patiently watching and waiting. He was aware he was in a vulnerable position lying where he was, but he had no other option. It was a waiting game.

Bodie's horse had moved off a number of yards. He could hear the creak of saddle-leather as it moved, searching for grass, air blowing through its nostrils.

Then he heard the tread of boot steps coming up behind him. Not one set. Two. The brush of clothing against the undergrowth. The added sound of led horses.

'Ol' Thad was right,' one of them said. 'That's one sly boy.'

'That's why he allus comes back alive,' the second man said. 'He don't trust nothin' 'cept hisself.'

The boot steps halted.

'Who you reckon he is?'

'Lawman. Maybe a bounty hunter. Sure won't be a friend 'cause Thad don't have any friends.'

One of them laughed. 'Right enough there. If'n it weren't for family Thad would be right lonely.'

'Hey, Cletus, you sure you hit this yahoo?'

'Yeah. Why?'

'I don't see no blood.'

'Don't make no fuss about it. Got him on the other side. He's done.'

'You reckon?'

'Just go get your piece 'fore we get too close.'

Bodie heard the drag of feet as one of them turned.

This is the time, he told himself. *Before they both have their hands filled with guns.*

He rolled over onto his back, hauling his upper body off the ground, the Colt in his big right hand already cocked as he sighted the two men.

They were ten, maybe twelve feet away.

The closest one faced him.

The second man had his back to Bodie as he moved towards his waiting horse, one hand reaching for the rifle jammed in a leather sheath.

The first man had his own weapon cradled in the crook of his arm and as Bodie moved he swung the rifle around, a wild yell bursting from his lips.

Bodie fired twice, the .45 slamming out heavy sound. He placed a slug in each knee. Blood, flesh and shattered bone misted the air as the big slugs blasted their way through the delicate kneecaps. The man, Cletus, screamed, staggered and fell, his rifle slipping from his grasp and he collapsed to the forest floor.

His partner yanked his rifle from the sheath, twisting his head as Bodie's shots echoed through the trees. He brought his rifle round, sliding his finger across the trigger as he frantically worked the lever.

Bodie two-handed the Peacemaker as he targeted the man. This time he made no attempt to wound. Two shots again. This time into the man's broad forehead, between the eyes, the solid slugs ripped into the man's skull, blowing out through the top of his head and taking off his hat in a shower of bloody debris. The man toppled over backwards, his finger jerking the trigger of his rifle and sending a .44–40 slug up through the branches.

Bodie pushed to his feet. The barrel of his revolver held on the kneecapped Cletus who was sitting hunched over, clutching his ruined, bleeding limbs, moaning against the pain. Crossing over Bodie kicked aside the man's rifle and threw away the heavy Dragoon Colt tucked behind his belt.

'*Sonofabitch, oh, you sonofabitch*,' the man screamed. 'You done crippled me. Shot out my goddamn knees.'

'Seeing as how you tried to back shoot me,' Bodie said, 'should I feel sorry for you?'

'*Bastard*. You were dogging Thad's trail. He's family. We protect our own. Had to be done.'

Bodie stood over the moaning man.

'Mister, that family man overreached himself this time. Three people shot dead so he could help himself to 8,000 dollars, and one of the dead was a young woman he shot in the back. This time he really went over the line.'

'He's still family.' Cletus's face twisted in a grimace of pain. 'Why didn't you just kill me?'

'I had me a notion to let you suffer.'

Bodie scooped up the man's weapons. He crossed to where the dead man lay and collected his guns. He wrapped them in the slicker he took from behind the saddle of the closest horse and tied them behind his own saddle. Then he stripped saddles and bridles from the two horses and chased them off.

'Hey, you sonofabitch, what about me? I ain't happy with what you're doin'.'

'Leaving you here to think about how you were ready to kill me is what I'm about to do.'

Cletus clutched his ruined knees, hands dripping with blood. He raised his head to stare at Bodie. His eyes were bright with rage.

'I get out of this,' he said, 'I'll track you to Hell and back. By God, you'll look round one day and I'll be walkin' after you for a reckoning.'

Bodie glanced at the man's bloody, smashed knees.

'Boy, you just won't have a leg to stand on for something like that.'

He mounted up and turned his horse back on the thin trail Monk had left behind. Letting his horse pick its way Bodie shucked out the empty brass shells and reloaded, filling all six chambers before he holstered the Colt. He felt damn sure he was going to be needing the weapon again — and soon.

He scanned the wide sky above the mountain peaks. Dark clouds were showing. That was all Bodie needed. A storm.

Then he thought about it. Maybe a rainstorm would help to hide his approach to Monk's place. Anything to give him an advantage was welcome.

If Thaddeus Monk was anything to go by the rest of the clan were likely to be the same. The two he had just clashed with had already shown they had little respect for anyone not part of the family. Bodie wondered just how many of them there were. If they were as close-knit a family as they seemed and followed the Bible's recommendations about begetting, there would be a fair number of them up on the mountain. Increasing their family numbers was obviously something they believed in, but loving their fellow man looked to be low on the list of priorities.

6

The second day out and Brand was well into the San Juans. He had negotiated the lower slopes and was moving into the tree line. There was an abundance of timber, and as he moved higher the stands grew denser. Grass and bushes were scattered among the trees. In all it was verdant terrain. Quiet, too, which didn't bother Brand at all.

It allowed him time to think about the son he had just acquired. Trouble was the more he thought about Adam, the more he had to admit to a degree of unease. He hadn't had much truck with young boys and especially one he had sired.

How, he wondered, did he handle Adam? Being a father was one hell of a responsibility. And Brand had no idea how to handle that responsibility. He had been one his own since his own teenage years. Actually from the day the Comanche had slaughtered his family he had been on his own. He had made his way into adult life and despite all the mistakes he'd made — and there had been a hell of lot of those — he was still alive. When he thought about it his past record didn't hold much of a promise for him becoming a good parent.

Brand leaned forward to stroke his horse's neck. Slipped off his hat and ran fingers through his dark hair. He felt the ridged scar there, courtesy of the Chinese, Kwo Han, who had almost ended Brand's life with a Tong hatchet. The wound had been the cause of Brand's memory loss. It had taken him a long time to recover. Brand jammed the hat back on and spurred the horse forward, his eyes constantly on the move as he searched the rising slopes.

Needle in a haystack came to mind.

The mountain range spread for miles in all directions.

McCord had told him it would be an

easy assignment to let him get a feeling for the job. The only feeling Brand was experiencing right then was the ache in his butt. He swung out of the saddle and led the chestnut for a while.

By the late afternoon Brand was becoming more than a little irritated with his lack of progress. He had to remind himself he was trying to find a couple of men in a hell of a lot of territory. His impatience came, not just through his lack of achievement, but from the realization he might be moving in the wrong direction. Traveling well away from where the two men might have been going. There were four points to the compass and the two men he was looking for — Calvin and Rankin — could have been moving in any one of those four directions.

Brand decided he'd had enough for one day. He spent another half hour searching for a place where he could bed down for the night. He chose a spot at the base of a rock face that showed through the trees. After seeing to his horse he made a small fire so he could boil water for coffee. He had hard biscuits and dried beef. Not the most palatable food, but then he wasn't on a picnic. He had a few of his thin cigars wrapped in a bundle and he lit one and settled back, resting against his saddle.

Inactivity forced him to think about Adam. It wasn't that he didn't want to. Brand was still accepting the fact. Not just a son but a nearly grown man. Thinking on it he decided he would rather have it that way than a youngster of nine or ten. At least Adam was of an age where he could fend for himself if the need arose.

When the need arose.

That need had come for Brand when his family had been killed, abandoned by the three working hands his father had hired, his sister taken by the Comanche where she had died. His choices had been non-existent. There had been no other way for him except to go out and avenge their deaths. Still a boy, untried, and walking in a man's world, where violence and betrayal had shadowed him. He had achieved his revenge in the end — but at what cost? When it was over he was still alone. His life stretching ahead of him and his only skill the gun in his hand . . .

Brand saw that his cigar had gone out and his mug of coffee was cold. The sun was already setting. He was no closer to solving the problem of his son, or the missing men.

'*Damnit to hell*,' he growled.

He tossed aside the dead cigar and threw out the coffee. He unrolled his blanket and pulled his slicker over it in case of rain. When he lay down he found sleep eluding him and lay staring into the coming darkness.

Come morning Brand woke stiff and in a sullen mood. He broke camp, packed his gear and saddled up. His horse was ready to go. It had obviously had a better night than him. He sawed its head around and thumped it with his heels. The chestnut protested until Brand hauled the reins up short. It did a frisky jig, stamping its hooves. Brand let it get rid of the steam.

'You feeling better now?' he asked when the horse settled down.

When he gigged the chestnut it moved off and Brand settled in the saddle. The horse blew air from its nostrils in a final moment of rebellion.

'Damn horses and women,' Brand said. 'Always got to have the last word.'

He rode for a hour, covering ground before it became too hot. Brand noticed the tree line was thinning out. Up ahead he could see open slopes.

He needed some kind of human contact. Someone who might be able to offer insight into where the two missing men might be. It was a notion, Brand thought. But maybe not something that would be easy to achieve. This was empty country. Isolated and the possibility of having folk wandering around . . .

He recalled the Marshal back in Santa Fe mentioning the homestead in the hills somewhere. If he could locate it he might gain some information. All he knew was it lay in the general area. At least it was a possibility. Vague. But at least it offered a chance. Brand had little else to go on. So he kept riding, searching. Listening, and sometime in the afternoon he picked up the unmistakable sound of a gunshot. A fair distance away. The sound echoed. Brand pinpointed the direction.

His earlier thoughts evaporated. It seemed he was not alone after all.

Brand followed the drift of sound as a few more shots sounded. He wondered who was firing on who. It might be someone out hunting. Going for deer. He dismissed that. The shooting had come from a rifle and a handgun and handguns were not much use when it came to hunting.

Unless it had been someone hunting a man.

Which seemed more than likely.

Brand slid his rifle from the boot, checked it and kept across the thighs as he pushed on.

It crossed his mind that the shooting might have been to do with the two men he was looking for.

Joseph Calvin.

Deputy Hec Rankin.

Sooner or later he was going to find out.

★ ★ ★

It happened to be sooner. A couple of miles on and he came across two men.

One was dead.

The other had both knees shot out, his blood soaking his pants around the messy wounds.

Brand sat studying the area. He saw two saddle and bridles where a pair of horses had been stripped. The hoof prints showed where the animals had run off. Then he spotted single horse tracks leading off from the shooting site, cutting off through the trees. The rider was following another single rider who had passed much earlier.

A groan attracted Brand's attention.

He glanced down at the kneecapped man. He was staring up at Brand, his face sheened with sweat. He raised a bloodied hand from one knee.

'You need to help me, mister,' Cletus whispered, his voice hoarse and ragged. 'That bastard shot me and rode off. Boogered the horses and just left me. I been here on my lonesome.'

Brand climbed out of the saddle, keeping his rifle close. He unhooked a canteen and passed it to the man. He watched Cletus uncap the canteen and take gulping swallows, spilling almost as much as he drank.

'What happened?'

Cletus suffered a coughing fit as he drank too much water. When the choking ceased he stared up at Brand.

'Sonofabitch done drygulched us,' he said. 'Snuck up on us and shot us. Ran off our rides. He killed Arnie. Left me to bleed to death.'

'*Why?*' Brand asked. 'He lookin' to rob you? He have some kind of grudge against you?'

Cletus took too long in answering. Brand could almost see his mind working on a plausible answer.

'*Yeah*. Never seen him before today. Must have been set to rob us . . . '

'He get anything?'

Pain creased the man's face and he sucked breath against it.

'*Get what?*' he asked, the hurt from his ruined knees dulling his response.

'You said he robbed you. What did he take?'

'We didn't have a thing to take.'

Brand felt a thread of suspicion grow. The assaulted men had been attacked by a stranger, out of nowhere, who had supposedly come to steal from them. They had nothing worth taking so the stranger had shot them, then ridden off. If the man had been attempting robbery why had he unsaddled their horses and run them off? The animals could have been worth a price but he had scattered them. And then there was the single line of horse tracks the ambusher had followed.

Something didn't sit right. The tale Cletus had handed out warned Brand there was more to the story.

'You near to home?' Brand asked. 'Somewhere I can ride to and get you help?'

'North. Up in the hills. People there are family.'

'How far?'

'Few hours.' Cletus rocked in pain. 'Damn it, man, you ain't about to leave me? I'm bad hurt.'

Brand crossed to where the dumped saddles and gear lay. He brought it all together. He used the saddle blankets to form a crude bed. Placed one saddle for a headrest. Ignoring Cletus's moans he manhandled him onto the blankets. He used his knife to cut shirts from the saddlebags to fashion bandages he bound around Cletus's bloody knees, then opened the blanket rolls and covered the man. All the time Cletus was grumbling and wincing with pain. Brand ignored him as he completed his work. In the saddlebags he found beef jerky and not surprisingly a couple of flat bottles of home-brewed liquor. He placed the items close to Cletus. There were some rough, handmade cigars in one pouch and a pack of matches.

'I'll swing by your place,' Brand said. 'Let your people know where you're at so they can come and get you. Best I can do. They got some kind of wagon up there?'

'Mebbe.'

'Only way to get you home,' Brand said. 'Those leg wounds need tending proper. Even doctoring. A wagon ride is what you need.' Brand stood over Cletus. 'I might have made up a travois but dragging you up this mountain would make those knees worse. You'd be bouncing around something cruel. Likely you'd suffer more blood loss and you already spilled too much.'

Cletus glowered up at him. He snatched up one of the bottles of liquor, jerked out the cork and took a swallow. The stuff was raw and strong and set him to coughing again. Tears formed in his eyes.

Brand unrolled the slickers he found with the saddles. He spread them out and covered Cletus.

'I ain't got no gun,' Cletus whined. 'Just recalled that bastard took ours.'

'Well I don't have one to spare,' Brand said.

He left the canteen of water alongside the other items.

'Hell of a way to leave a man,' Cletus said. 'I could die out here.'

Brand caught the inflection in his words. The accusation.

'Let's hope you're wrong,' Brand said.

'Name's Cletus Monk. I want you to remember it, mister. We could be meeting again.'

That was enough to jerk Brand into motion. He mounted up and set his horse on the clear trail left by the other two riders. There were questions crowding him now. Concerning the man who had clashed with Cletus

Monk and had trailed after another, as yet unknown, rider. A great deal had occurred hereabouts and none of it made a much sense. Whatever lay ahead, it didn't promise much in the way of peace and quiet.

Behind him Brand could hear Cletus doing some considerable cursing himself, his voice breaking the mountain silence. The man appeared to have a disagreeable nature, his wounds apart. Brand found himself wondering if the rest of his kin were like-minded. He hoped not.

The tracks he followed meandered for mile or so, then settled into a clear direction. The man at the head of the trail plainly knew where he was going. And from the way he was traveling it appeared it was in the same general direction as Brand.

Brand disliked complications. When he had started out his assignment seemed clear enough. Find the missing men and work out what had happened to them. Bring them out of the mountains if they were still alive. Now the whole affair had taken a sudden turn. He was no closer to finding out where Calvin and Rankin were. Finding the wounded man, Cletus, had added to Brand's burden. He had promised to ride to the man's home and let his family know where Cletus was. That had seemed simple enough. But now he had two unknown men riding ahead of him. One seemingly trailing the other. And they were riding in the same general direction as Brand. It was possible their paths would cross. The fact that Cletus had been shot and left for dead gave Brand cause for concern.

Who was he following?

Another lawman?

Or a loose gun?

Brand sighed. Fate. Bad luck. Whatever it was called, it had a habit of showing up and adding a twist to what had appeared a simple enough search. It wasn't the first time unexpected events conspired to alter matters.

What was it McCord had said?

A simple enough assignment. An easy way to get back into his job.

Complications had already come in the shape of his son. Adam's appearance had been something Brand could never have expected. Yet it had happened and however complicated Brand had figured his life to be, the boy showing up had thrown everything else out the window.

Now he had this odd mix of events to deal with.

Brand hadn't asked for it. Yet there it was and he was going to have to handle it.

7

Adam had followed Brand's trail with ease. Even when they moved into the timbered slopes the hoof prints stayed fresh enough to be able to spot. Back home Adam had been friendly with an old Kiowa who had spent some years as a scout for the army and now hung around town picking up work wherever he could. The Indian had taken to the younger man and they had spent many hours riding free, Adam listening as his friend gave him instructions on how to pick up and follow tracks. The advice was proving to be handy now as Adam followed his father up into the hills.

He had felt bad sneaking out of Santa Fe, knowing that Emilio would be worried when he realized the boy had gone. The man at the livery would eventually tell what had happened. How he had hired out a horse and gear to the young man. There was little they could do. No way they could warn Brand. Adam had left a brief note for Emilio, explaining his intentions, and for the man not to worry.

Emilio would be upset.

And Adam's father would be angry when he found out.

In the end Adam didn't care. He had only just found his father and he had no intentions of losing him. Too many years had gone by and Adam wanted to be a part of his father's life now.

He had sneaked into the hotel kitchen and had taken a supply of food, leaving some money along with the note he'd written. He fastened the sack across the back of the saddle of the horse he'd rented from the livery, had taken a looping ride away from town before picking up Brand's tracks and had settled in for the long ride ahead.

Brand had been gone almost a day when Adam rode out. Impatience had fuelled his determination to go. He pushed the horse firmly, wanting to make up some distance, and had cut the gap considerably by the second day.

The trail led up through the foothills, eventually into heavy timber. By the second day out Adam was climbing the slopes of the looming mountains. The day was bright, the landscape thick with trees and brush. There was a pervading silence. The only sound came from his own passing and the chatter of birds flitting back and forth through the foliage. When he stopped to rest his horse and eat he was beside a tumbling clear stream that rushed down from the higher slopes. He let the horse drink and feed itself on the plentiful grass edging the water. He used his knife to hack off a chunk of the cooked beef he'd taken from Emilio's kitchen along with a freshly baked loaf. The stream provided cold water and he refilled his canteen before he moved on. He allowed an hour to rest before he mounted and turned the horse back on the trail.

The horse was a black mare with a

wide white strip running down from between her ears. When Adam had ridden away from Santa Fe he had found the animal frisky and had to apply a firm hand. The mare offered some resistance at first, but when she realized the rider was no beginner she settled down and as they rose higher up the mountain slopes proved herself to be a sturdy, determined animal.

His solitary ride allowed Adam ample time to work out what he would say when he located his father. Brand would be angry that his son had gone against his wishes. Adam hoped he would be able to explain his actions. It was simply that he needed to be with his father. Since the death of his mother he had been alone. That did not reflect on his Uncle. The man had treated Adam as if he had been his own, but as much as he respected the man, Adam always felt a stranger in the man's house. He couldn't explain it any more than that. He had known he had a father somewhere, and there was always that need to find him. To confront the man. Brand had never been told of Adam's existence. Adam felt he had a right to know. And truth be told he had always carried the need to meet his father. He had not been disappointed when he had finally stood face to face with Brand. What he had learned from Alex Mundy had already given him an impression of what Brand would look like, and in reality the tall, broad-shouldered figure had lived up to his expectations. Brand's character had been a little intimidating to the younger man. He was strong-willed. Said exactly what he thought and made no bones about the fact Adam's presence had caught him at a difficult time.

Adam understood, too, that his own attitude had not exactly helped. He quickly realized he had inherited Brand's impatience and a stubborn streak. He couldn't help that. It was part of him and was behind the impulsive act that had brought him here, to this mountain slope, where he was searching for his father. In the short time he had been close to Brand, Adam had become aware of his father's strong character. His way with words and the strong way he expressed himself.

'Horse,' he said, 'he's going to give me hell when I show my face.' The thought made him smile. 'I mean what can he do? *Shoot me?*'

The mare made a soft sound that sounded to Adam that it was agreeing with him.

He found a place to make camp as the day ended. He ate. Drank water before he settled his horse, then rolled himself in his blankets and slept through until first light.

Now his way took him across a shallow swell of ground that brought him to a bare ridge. He drew rein and scanned the way ahead. No movement, except for the sway of trees and the grass. Adam saw gathering clouds to the north and east. They looked heavy, swollen with rain, and he picked up the still-distant rumble of thunder. He sat for a while, studying the weather signs. There was a storm on the way and it was heading in his direction. He felt a rise in the wind. It was starting to build. Even the black sensed the weather change as it pricked up its ears.

'That is all I need,' Adam said. 'Horse, we are going to get wet pretty soon.'

The other disadvantage with a storm coming was the likelihood of it washing away any tracks he was following. He pushed the horse forward, picking up the pace, keeping one eye on the weather signs and the other on the tracks he was following.

8

Bodie had been watching the storm clouds heading his way and didn't like what he saw. It was threatening to be one hell of a blow. He reached behind to loosen the ties holding his oilskin slicker behind the saddle. He laid it across the horse's neck in front of him in case he needed it. The wind came first, drifting in from the higher peaks to disturb the tops of the closely packed trees. Within a half hour the wind had risen. It picked up loose leaves from the forest floor and scattered them around. Bodie felt his horse jerk as the disturbed leaves floated in front of him. He tightened his reins and told the horse to quit fooling around.

The first drops of rain came down through the swaying branches, cold against Bodie's face. Staring up through the trees Bodie saw the sheeting mist of rain come down off the peaks, dark against the sky. He saw the shifting pattern as it rolled in and moments later the deluge came. It all arrived at the same time. The heavy rain and the hard wind. And far back in the mountain peaks the deep rumble of thunder.

As Bodie pulled on the slicker, dragging the folds down to cover himself, he decided it was turning into one hell of a miserable day. He could feel the force of the downpour through the slicker across his back. He tugged his hat low against the slap of the rain against his face. Beneath him the gray shivered in reaction to the inclement weather; it didn't think much of the sudden downpour and the wind.

'No use making a fuss, horse,' Bodie said. 'This is what we got. I don't favor it too much myself.'

He angled across the slope as the tracks ahead veered in that direction. Bodie realized the tracks would be lost soon enough. The forest floor was already soaked and given time would become pretty well waterlogged. If the storm stayed for a time the natural streams would become filled as water running off the slopes reached them. Bodie dismounted and led the gray. On foot he was able to pick up the faint trail easier. His boots sank into the ground where it was already sodden.

Off on the high peaks thunder rolled in. A rising sound that reverberated from the gray skies. Bodie's horse pulled against the reins and he had to jerk it back on line. The deep sound continued for a time. Bodie hoped, peevishly, Monk was getting just as wet. He wouldn't have liked to believe the man had found shelter.

Just when he thought he had lost Monk's trail Bodie picked up faint hoof prints. He squatted, checking the marks in the soft earth. He followed the prints as they kept on a direct line for the higher slopes.

'We ain't lost him yet, hoss,' he said.

Bodie turned to remount. As he did

he caught movement out the corner of his eye.

A lone rider on a lower slope, moving in a parallel line to Bodie's. There must have been at least close on a half mile distance between them. The other rider seemed to be moving slowly and the only reason Bodie could put on that was the man appeared to be searching his way ahead. Almost as if he was looking for someone himself — or looking for something. Bodie watched the rider until he was swallowed by a dense thicket of brush.

Studying the rider, even at a distance, told Bodie the man was not Thad Monk. Monk's description had him on the short, heavily built side. Sitting his saddle the distant rider was taller and leaner than Monk.

Bodie swung his horse around to follow the tracks he had found. The way took him into more trees, the falling shadows making a crisscross pattern on the ground. He kept the gray to a slow walk, scanning the way ahead.

He was curious about the newcomer. His identity. His reason for being where he was. Bodie's instinct told him the man was not associated with Monk, or his kin. He could be wrong about that, but Bodie had a feeling he was right. Even so the man needed to be watched. He did have as much right to be up here in the mountainous country as did Bodie. The land was open and free to travel and this rider could have a perfectly legitimate reason for being here.

Until he found out, one way or the other, Bodie decided to keep an open — albeit cautious — mind. It paid a man to take care in this wild country. In most cases one mistake was all it took. A dead man was not allowed a second chance and Bodie had not survived for so long by not taking anything for granted. A bullet in the back tended to end all questions.

9

The closer he got to his destination the edgier Brand became. The feeling he had over the whole affair was making itself known to him. There was too much that hadn't been explained to his satisfaction. It made Brand accept he was still not fully recovered from his enforced sabbatical. Maybe he should have refused McCord's placing him back on the active list. The odd thing was he felt physically fine. It was his inner self that still held him back. And forced him to question things.

The man, Cletus, had given him an explanation that dogged Brand's thoughts. He was beginning to doubt the man's story. Yet here he was, about to ride into the unknown. By placing himself at the mercy of the man's family Brand was leaving himself exposed.

One man was dead. Cletus wounded and pushing an explanation Brand found suspect. So where did that leave him?

The abrupt change in the weather had only added to Brand's discomfort. The long weeks of recovery had taken the edge off his resistance. A storm like this one would never have worried him previously. Right now he was cold and a touch damp, having been caught by the downpour before he could pull on his slicker to cover his coat. That had done little to temper his mood.

It was close to midday. He had been riding long enough to be near the location Cletus had outlined for him. The fact revealed itself when he saw a partially tended field of crops. Corn stalks were bending under the downpour. Brand drew rein and studied the field. At the far side he made out a broken pole fence. There were a number of tree stumps. Felled trees leaving an open aspect. Signs of human presence.

Brand rode on, skirting the edge of the field and on the far side he topped a slight rise in the land and found himself looking down on a collection of buildings. A couple of barns. Outhouses. A wide stable and corrals. And to one side a large timber house. The additions to the original building had been added to over a number of years. That was evident in the newness of some of the extensions compared to the weathered main house. Smoke issued from chimneys, whipped away by the wind and rain. Brand saw no movement. Whoever lived here was staying out of the weather.

'Let's do this,' he said and gigged the chestnut forward.

The yard was muddy and puddles were dotted here and there. Brand hauled up in front of the porch and slid his right hand under the slicker, gripping the Colt.

'Anyone at home?' Brand raised his voice above the storm sound. 'Hey.'

He caught sight of movement behind

one of the house windows. The main door rattled as it was opened. It was a large, heavy structure. As it swung wide Brand spotted more movement behind another window and saw the gleam of lamplight on metal as a weapon was raised.

The figure planted in the open door was big. A solid, wide-shouldered man, bracing one large hand against the frame of the door.

'You picked a hell of a day to come calling,' the man said. 'What's your business?'

'This the home of Cletus Monk?'

'Mebbe so, mebbe not.'

The man stepped forward, his lined face shadowed by a growth of beard. His clothes were those of a farmer. Most likely homespun. He carried no weapon.

'I came across Cletus Monk down the mountain,' Brand said. 'He's been shot. Both knees. Another feller with him was dead. I did what I could for Cletus. Bound his wounds and made him comfortable. He's got food and drink. Blankets. No way I could fetch him home. I said I'd find his place so his people could take a wagon bring him back.' Brand paused. 'So am I in the right place?'

'I'm Nathaniel Monk. Cletus is my boy.'

'He told me they were attacked by some stranger. Ran off their horses before he left.'

'World is full of evil doers,' Monk said. 'That's why we built our home here. Away from harm.'

Brand shifted in his saddle. 'Looks to me it found you.'

'And you, stranger. What brings you up here?'

'Lookin' for couple of missing fellers,' Brand said. 'You ain't had any visitors recently?'

Nathaniel Monk's change of expression told Brand the man knew what he was referring to. He covered it quickly, shaking his head.

'Can't say . . . '

His denial came too quickly. Cut off when his eyes flickered to Brand's left. A second before the hard muzzle of a rifle was jammed against Brand's side.

'Another lawdog,' a voice said close by. 'Damn it, pa, I smelled him right off.'

Another?

That meant something to Brand. Hec Rankin maybe?

Brand stayed silent. It seemed the right thing to do under the circumstances.

'Down off the horse, lawdog, and keep your hand away from the gun under that slicker.'

The rifle muzzle was pushed harder against Brand's ribs to emphasize the suggestion. He climbed down off the chestnut, exposing his right hand in the process. The prodding rifle stayed against his side the whole time.

Nathaniel Monk was at the edge of the porch, watching Brand closely.

'That the case, mister? You law?'

'It going to make a difference?'

The man with the rifle gave a harsh chuckle. He moved so he came into Brand's eyesight. A thickset man with a coarse-featured, unshaven face. His eyes held an unhealthy gleam.

'Hell, boy, it could mean all the difference in the world. Now get yourself inside the house so's we can all take a look at you. And think on — we don't take kindly to lawdogs.'

Brand made his way past the elder Monk and stepped inside the house. The prodding rifle muzzle never eased away from Brand.

'Take the slicker off.'

Brand removed the dripping cape. It was snatched away by a skinny, wild-eyed younger man who grinned at Brand, showing large teeth.

'He's got a gun,' the man said excitedly.

Nathaniel Monk reached and took away the Colt.

'Rafe, search him,' he said.

Rafe pulled open Brand's coat, dragged it from his shoulders and threw it down. He saw the shoulder-holstered revolver. He snatched it clear, holding it up so everyone could see it.

Brand felt the rifle withdrawn from his spine. The man holding it moved so he could face Brand. He reached for the cut-down Colt, examining it with interest.

'Now ain't that a pretty sight,' he said. 'That is one hideaway hogleg.'

'Give it to me,' Nathaniel said. 'Give it to me now, Rafe.'

Rafe Monk handed over the Colt, muttering under his breath.

Nathaniel examined it, turning the weapon over as he checked the neat conversion, appreciating the way it had been altered.

'Man who did this has a love of guns,' he murmured.

Brand took a moment to examine the large, low-ceilinged room and its occupants. A large timber table stood in the center, with benches on either side and a large single chair at the head. To his right was a massive stone fireplace with logs burning in the hearth. He could smell the wood smoke. Beyond the fireplace an open way showed a kitchen. A wooden staircase led to the upper floor. The whole room was cluttered with possessions. Whatever else they were the Monks, as a family, were far from organized.

He counted eight, maybe nine people. Two were women. They returned his stare without a moment of interest, turning away to go back to whatever they had been doing. Brand noticed a subservient manner in the way they reacted. He got the feeling they were not exactly happy where they were.

The men moved across the room to crowd him.

'Ease off, boys,' Nathaniel said, his attention diverted from the Colt. 'Don't crowd our guest. We should show him some consideration, seeing as how he made a special trip to tell us about Cletus. That was the act of a Good Samaritan.' He thrust a large fist out, finger extended. 'Couple of you break out the wagon. Hitch up a team and go fetch Cletus and his brother to home. And take this man's horse into the stable. No weather for one of God's creatures to be left standing on its own.' His voice rose to a boom of sound. 'Now, I say. Move your lazy asses.'

Two of the men broke from the bunch. They located heavy coats and hats and stomped out of the house.

Two less, Brand thought. *The odds are reducing.*

'Mister, I see a gleam in your eye I don't like,' Nathaniel said. 'There a notion in your mind to turn against us? You watch him close, Rafe.'

One of the group stepped forward, his eyes raking Brand from head to foot.

'Pa, he's a lawdog,' the man said. 'Man's a lawdog, and lawdogs will go against us every time.'

The one called Rafe was jigging about near Brand, his eyes wild with excitement.

'You want me to smite him, pa? Just like you read us from the book?'

'Shut your mouth, loon,' the other man said. 'Any smiting needs doin' I can deliver that.'

'Seems to me,' Nathaniel said, 'this man should be repaid for bringing us news about Cletus. He's looking for his friends. He should know they're here as our guests. Nolan, take him to see them. Let them spend time together. When the storm runs out he can go to work with them.'

Nolan grinned and Rafe hooted with laughter.

'Good thinking, pa,' Nolan said. 'One more pair of hands.' He leveled his rifle at Brand. 'Move it, boy. Let's go meet you friends.'

Brand was escorted through the house to a heavy door at the rear. Rafe drew the iron bolts back and swung the door open.

Nolan slammed his big hand between Brand's shoulders and pushed him forward into the room beyond.

'You were lookin' for these boys?' he said. 'Go say hello.'

The door slammed shut behind Brand.

Well, son, you sure went and walked into this one, Brand thought. *Let's see how easy you get out.*

10

Bodie's line of travel took him higher across the slopes. It was a couple of hours since he had seen the other rider. There was no more sign of the man. It was not surprising. The heavy clouds overhead effectively cut down on the light reaching down through the trees. It was like an early twilight.

Despite Bodie's strong hand on the reins his horse remained spooked by the thunder and the occasional lightning flashes. The horse pulled to the right, stepping awkwardly as its hoofs came into contact with water-sodden, spongy ground. Bodie felt its balance go. He pulled on the reins but the powerful animal ignored his move and gave a shrill squeal. The gray faltered, desperately trying to pull itself upright. Bodie realized it was going down. He slipped his feet from the stirrups, still trying to drag the animal upright, but the sheer bulk of the horse overrode his attempts. It uttered another panicked cry as its right foreleg collapsed under the strain. As it fell Bodie rolled out of the saddle, throwing out his hands as he dropped. He landed on his left side, making an attempt to control his fall. The rain-sodden ground partly cushioned his fall, but he still landed hard, breath driven from his lungs by the impact. He slithered through the muddy grass, aware the ground was dropping away. There was a rushing sound in his ears and he only realized what it was seconds before he was plunged into the cold rush of water. A heavy runoff. Water that was rushing down out of the higher slopes in a tumbling stream.

Bodie struggled to resist the pull of the water. It was his heavy slicker pulling him down as it folded itself around him. For long seconds he was dragged under the surface, water spilling into his mouth. He fought the cling of the slicker, pulling it up over his head as he was turned and twisted by the water. His head cleared the surface and he spat out water, sucking in precious air, still attempting to extricate himself from the slicker. His hat went as he dragged the oilskin folds clear. The slicker floated away, leaving Bodie sucking in air and kicking for the bank of the runoff. It was only feet away but it could have been further. He felt solid ground under his boots, pushed hard and propelled himself towards the bank. His grasping fingers caught a handful of grass. The moment he put his weight on it the grass tore free and he was thrust further down the foaming stream.

He saw the exposed roots of a tree that leaned over the stream as he was swept towards it. He would have one chance. Bodie threw out a hand, his fingers scraping against the slick root. He grasped it. Held tight, fighting the pull of the water. After a few seconds he closed his other hand over the root and began to haul himself out of the water. It fought to retain its grasp on him, swinging his body back and forth, but his not inconsiderable strength won out and inch by inch Bodie dragged himself onto hard ground. He rolled on his back, staring up through the trees as he sucked in air.

The moment he thought about it Bodie dropped his right hand to his side, fingers finding the butt of his Colt. The hammer loop had prevented the weapon from slipping from the holster. When he checked his left side he found his sheathed knife was still there.

Bodie sat up. He could feel the pound of the rain on his back. The distant rumble of thunder. He brushed his hair back from his face.

'I liked that hat,' he muttered as he pushed to his feet, turning back to retrace his way to where he had come off his horse.

His concern for the animal was justified when he found it. On its left side, eyes rolling, it thrashed about, unable to right itself. The first thing he checked was its right leg. Bone showed through the torn flesh. Bodie slipped the Colt from the holster as he moved to stand over the gray. He'd had the horse for some considerable time.

'Why'd you have to go and do that,' he said softly.

The gray stared up at him, quiet now, almost as if it understood.

Sonofabitch.

Bodie pulled the hammer back. The sound of the shot was loud in the forest, the echo briefly drowning out the rainfall. The gray convulsed, then lay still.

Bodie didn't concern himself his shot might be heard by others. Leaving the gray suffering was not something he could have done. He could have used his knife but cutting the animal's throat could have been messy and caused the horse more suffering. It had been the quickest way to put the animal down and Bodie figured that was the least he could have done.

Bodie slid his Winchester from the scabbard. He managed to drag his saddlebags free and draped them over his left shoulder. His canteen was crushed under the horse's body along with Bodie's blanket roll and the guns he had taken earlier but Bodie considered that no great loss.

He stood for a while, fixing his position.

He was afoot, a distance from anywhere, so Bodie figured he might as well stay on the trail he had been following. Turning back was a notion that didn't even register. He still had a man to find. Thaddeus Monk. The bounty was still open for collection and Bodie was going to need a portion of that money to outfit himself again. If nothing else, the manhunter possessed a practical train of thought.

He was a man who didn't accept giving up. Not when he was on the hunt.

It was what had earned him the title given by other men.

The Stalker.

It was who he was.

What he did.

Better than most.

He settled the saddlebags, hefted the rifle, and moved off.

* * *

The slopes rose higher above him. Bodie could believe he'd hit the peaks if he kept on going.

'Monk, enjoy your freedom while you can, because I'm still coming to get you.'

Head down against the rain Bodie spent a couple minutes placing his position until he located the tracks, growing fainter by the minute, and moved on. On foot his pace matched that of his horse. He had been moving slowly before the fall, so even on foot he was able to maintain his travel. And being on foot meant he was closer to the ground, allowing him to keep the tracks in view.

Over the years his profession as a tracker had given him an unerring skill. He was using that skill now and it let him follow Cletus Monk's trail. By now he had adjusted to the downpour to the point it didn't bother him any longer. He simply kept moving, eyes searching, missing nothing. A deep hoof print where Monk's horse had left a mark in a patch of earth. The print was filled with water now, but the outline was still visible. A little further and Bodie spotted broken shrubbery where Monk's horse had pushed its way through a thick stand of greenery. The ends of the broken tendrils were still raw, the branches snapped in the direction of Monk's travel. He patiently followed the trail through a close grove of timber where the overhead canopy had kept most of the rainfall away. Here the mossy forest floor was damp but not overly waterlogged. Monk's passage was clearly marked. The man had been riding slow, but steady. His horse was walking, its hoof prints closer than if it had been moving quickly. Monk had stopped here, taking time to light himself a smoke. Bodie saw the spent wooden match he had used.

He allowed himself a slow smile. Monk was becoming casual. Figuring he was out of trouble and most likely getting closer to home.

Just stay that way, Bodie thought. *Keep telling yourself you're home free.*

He adjusted the saddlebags over his shoulder and walked on, emerging from the timber and faced an undulating stretch of the slope, backed by the high peaks. Bodie saw the sky was clearing, the storm clouds moving off to the east. Within the next half hour the rainfall slackened, then tapered off, the steady breeze chasing the last of the fall. Watery sunlight broke through as the storm petered out. It was not unusual with storms in the high country. They came on quickly and blew themselves out just as fast.

Movement caught Bodie's eye. He

swung the rifle to his shoulder, then relaxed as a pair of deer emerged from the trees off to his left. They saw him and froze. Bodie was moving away from them and they must have sensed he was no threat as they carried on their way.

Monk's trail was steady now. No deviation as he continued to ride in a direct line. The tracks he left now were clearer as the rain drained away and the forest floor firmed up over the next couple of hours. Bodie was able to keep on the trail. He moved easily, content to let Monk show him the way. It told Bodie his quarry was getting closer to home.

And the closer he got the more relaxed he would become. Being on familiar ground would boost Monk's confidence. The man was already relaxing, his tracks allowing Bodie to follow easily.

Bodie heard the wagon a while before he saw it. Pulled by a pair of horses, the flat bed held a couple of armed men. He crouched in the undergrowth and watched it pass some distance away, heading down the slope. Bodie watched until it was out of sight.

He eased from cover and kept moving. Something told him he was not far from his destination.

He came on the first sign of habitation and hour later. A wide field, planted with crops. Cut-down trees and a sagging fence. Then he saw the spread. House, barns. Stable and corrals. A big house, smoke rising from chimneys. He saw horses in the corrals. It was a substantial outfit. But nothing fancy.

He shucked his saddlebags at the base of a tree and headed for the main house, across the field fronting the wide yard. Bodie stayed in as much cover as he could, moving closer. He bellied down on the inside of the last fence bordering the place, partly concealed by the poles of the fence. He studied the place. Watching and waiting while he checked it out.

There was movement at the front

door as a figure stepped outside and lingered in the porch. Bodie focused on the man. The broad, heavyset figure was wearing a pair of matching revolvers in a double rig and had a rifle in his hands. The weapons were in contrast to the clothes the man wore. He was dressed in the rough, handmade outfit of a field hand: denim bib and brace overalls and heavy work boots. A thick wool shirt.

What interested Bodie more was the man's face. Bodie only had a wanted poster describing Thaddeus Monk. The man he was looking at bore a striking resemblance to the man who had robbed and killed. He had the same characteristics as Thaddeus Monk. He was younger. His face looked as if he hadn't yet shaved. And Thaddeus had a deep scar over his right eye.

So this was not Bodie's quarry. But it convinced Bodie he was in the right place. The problem now was figuring out how many others were inside the house. With the run of bad luck he was currently having Bodie figured there would most likely be a hell of a brood inside the house. A whole litter of Thaddeus Monk's relatives.

The man on the porch leaned the rifle aside and started playing with the holstered revolvers, a toothy grin on his face as he gripped the pistols and yanked them out. He began to twirl them on his fingers, chuckling to himself until the one in his left hand slipped from his grasp and fell to the porch. The man muttered to himself, bent to pick the gun up. Bent over, his eye level suddenly became in line with Bodie, who had tried to avoid being seen.

It was too late.

For a split second Bodie and the man locked stares.

Sonofabitch.

The man on the porch let out a loud yell and kept yelling.

But instead of retreating to the house, he snatched up the fallen revolver and started firing with both weapons.

Wood splinters blew across Bodie's face. He felt the sting as flesh was burned and rolled away from the fence, with the realization he had little cover behind him, and bad a shot as he was the kid was going to get lucky sooner or later.

Bodie felt the stinging burn as one of the .45 slugs sliced his left shoulder.

He pushed to one knee, risking revealing himself, and snapped the Winchester into position.

The sight of his target aiming back at him made the shooter pause for a heartbeat. It was all the time Bodie needed. He snugged the rifle butt against his shoulder, aimed, and fired. The Winchester's 44–40 bullet, with its 217-grain load, delivered a powerful shot. The slug slammed into the shooter's left shoulder, spinning him around and bouncing him off the timber wall behind him. The kid screamed from the solid impact, blood and flesh spurting from the exit wound. He dropped his guns and went down on his knees, his screams increasing.

With his opponent out of action Bodie pushed to his feet and doubled back across the field. He heard the clatter of feet on the porch as yelling figures burst from the house. Seconds later a burst of gunfire filled the air and cut close around Bodie's weaving figure. Pursuit would follow and Bodie needed to gain distance before he stood and faced the hostile Monk family.

He managed a faint and mocking thought.

He was the Stalker.

So why the hell was he the one doing the running away?

It might have been funny — if it hadn't been so damned serious.

As he hit the tree line the solid thwack of slugs ripping into the timber followed, Bodie dropped to a crouch, swinging around to face his pursuers.

Three of them. All armed, and blasting away with the rifles they were carrying. Wood chips and bark exploded around Bodie. He shouldered the Winchester, picked a target and placed a slug into the man's chest, splintering rib bones and driving them into the heart. As the man dropped Bodie shifted aim and hit a second target, the 44–40 lead slug ripping its way through flesh and bone, kicking the man off his feet. He was knocked back by the impact, his own weapon spinning from his grasp as he went down.

The surviving man turned about and went across the muddy field in panic. Bodie settled the Winchester and put a slug into one thigh, the impact tearing flesh and leaving a bloody wound. Bodie saw the man stumble as his leg gave way, plunging face down in the sodden dirt.

He picked up the sound of raised voices, caught sight of figures moving out from the house. More of them.

How many were there?

Bodie didn't stay to count the numbers. He made a grab for the saddlebags he'd dropped on his way in and headed back into the timber.

He had the feeling the whole Monk clan was going to be on his trail before long. One way or another he had poked a stick into a hornet's nest and they were coming after him.

11

Light filtered in from a barred window ten feet off the floor. Brand took a quick look around and saw he was in a twenty-foot square room. It had a hard packed dirt floor, no furniture and two occupants who watched Brand in silence.

They were unshaven and their faces and clothes were dirt-streaked. Under the dirt their faces showed cuts and bruises. They sat on the floor, backs against one of the walls, hands resting on their upraised knees.

Brand tipped back his hat and faced the pair.

'*Hec Rankin?*'

The leaner of the pair raised a grimy hand.

'Do I know you?' he said.

'I spoke to Marshal Dembrow back in Santa Fe. Told me where you were heading.' Brand jerked a thumb at the other man. 'You'd be Calvin?'

The second man nodded.

'I was sent to find you both,' Brand said. 'Looks like I found you but not the way I expected to.'

'You the law?' Calvin asked, licking at dry, cracked lips.

'You could say that.'

Rankin leaned forward, a hard expression in his eyes. 'You a damned bounty hunter?'

Brand squatted on his heels in front of them, shaking his head. 'My department doesn't go in for badges and such, but it's official. I don't carry papers.'

'*Sonofabitch*,' Rankin said. 'I heard about you fellers. You work from Washington?'

Brand nodded.

'What does that mean?' Calvin asked.

'Kind of an undercover lawman,' Rankin said. 'I heard talk about it. But I never met anyone from it.'

'Name's Brand.'

'Hell, I know *that* name too. You used to be a US Marshal. Right?'

'Few years back now.'

'They made you quit. Said you were giving the service a bad reputation.'

'Like I said it's history.'

'Damn shame,' Rankin said. 'You did your job. Got results. So why . . . ?'

'Killed a feller who drew a knife on me. Couldn't prove it. The knife disappeared. Feller I shot was a Senator's son. His friends covered for him. The Senator knew people . . . '

Brand let the words trail off. There was no more to say. It had happened and he had moved on.

Calvin said, 'So they sent you to find us and bring us home?'

'That's the way of it. Me being in here with you is all part of my big plan to get you free.'

Hec Rankin gave a hoarse chuckle.

'So what's all this about?' Brand asked. 'You pair look like you been rolling around in the dirt for a while.'

'About a mile or so up the mountain

114

is a hole in the rock,' Rankin said. 'A cave leading to a tunnel. At the end of the tunnel is a vein of pure gold. Joe and me have been working that face since the Monks decided we were free labor.'

'True enough,' Calvin agreed. 'They've struck a big deposit. Enough to make them extremely rich. They want to keep it for themselves. Problem is the surrounding strata is unstable. Makes mining a risky proposition. In the time we've been forced to work the mine there have been a number of cave-ins. Two others were killed.'

'We got one out and buried him,' Rankin said. 'The other poor feller we just had to leave.'

'The Monks work the mine?'

Rankin shook his head. 'They just stand watch over us. Stay back far enough so they're safe. They take the ore when we pass it back and move it out the mine. Must have some place they store it but we have no idea.'

'Sounds they have it all worked out,' Brand said.

Calvin hunched his shoulders, his face pale and drawn.

'And there's nothing we can do about it.'

'Don't let yourself think that way.'

'Brand, you sound like a man who doesn't consider giving up,' Rankin said.

'Kind of something I don't cotton to,' Brand said. 'Female acquaintance calls it my stubborn nature.'

'She got you pegged?'

'Oh, yeah, she does.'

Rankin managed a grin at that. 'They figure you out every time.'

'How many guns we up against here?' Brand asked.

'Ain't easy to figure. Way I see it there are Monks all over this part of the mountain. Hell of a big family. So I can't tell you a number.'

'Sooner or later,' Brand said, 'I guess we'll have a chance to find out . . . '

12

Bodie heard the crackle of under-growth as a rider pushed his horse forward. There was a blurred image filling his vision. It loomed larger as the rider urged the animal forward, a wild yell as he spotted his quarry. Bodie half-turned as the rider leaned forward in his saddle, rifle coming into play. A shot would bring the rest of the Monks fast. Bodie let his rifle fall to the ground. He took a couple of lunging steps, digging in his heels as he launched himself forward. His out-stretched arms gripped the rider around his lower body, pushing him back out of the saddle. Bodie's forward motion took him over the horse's bulk and he followed the rider off the horse. They fell, hitting the ground hard, and then, without warning their scrambling bodies were falling into empty space.

The thick undergrowth they crashed through was edging a steep dropoff. Bodie and the Monk rider went over, still struggling, as the ground fell away in a long, deep slope. They were unable to control their descent, rolling and crashing down the muddy incline until they hit bottom, sinking into a wide spill of water. The water was a couple of feet deep, with thick, soft mud underneath.

They gained their feet together, spitting the brackish water from their mouths. Bodie saw the rider had lost his rifle during the fall. He had no handgun, but carried a sheathed knife. He went for it and lunged at Bodie, the gleam of the broad-bladed knife in his right hand. Bodie reared back as the knife cut the air, felt it tear at his shirt. Before the other man could recover Bodie reached out and grabbed his wrist, forcing the knife aside and swinging his bunched right fist in a powerful blow that connected with the Monk man's jaw. The blow was heavy, delivered with all of Bodie's strength. The man's head snapped to one side, blood streaking his flesh from a torn lip. Using the moment Bodie twisted the man's arm until he let go of the knife with a pained yell. It vanished under the muddy water.

'*Sonofabitch.*'

The man spat out the word, swinging his fists as he fought back. Bodie caught a glancing blow to his cheek. Felt warm blood seeping from the split flesh. He saw a second punch coming and ducked under the swing, driving forward to slam his own fist into the other's gut. There was a lot of energy in the punch. Enough to halt the man as his breath was driven from his lungs. Given the moment Bodie used it well, sledging in left and right blows to his opponent's jaw. Blood sprayed in a red mist as the punches landed, drawing a stunned grunt from the man. He toppled over and went face down in the water.

Straddling him Bodie planted both hands on the exposed skull and pushed the head down into the slick of water and mud, his weight preventing the man from raising himself clear. Bubbles of air exploded from around the submerged head. Bodie kept the pressure on until the man's struggles weakened, then hauled him up.

Gasping and spitting the Monk man fell into a spasm of harsh coughing. He offered little resistance when Bodie snaked one arm around his neck and held tight.

'Where's Thaddeus Monk?'

'Go to hell.'

'Wrong answer.'

Bodie shoved the man's head back into the muddy water and repeated the procedure. The man flailed, legs kicking. When Bodie pulled him clear again his face was streaked with mud.

'Where's Monk?'

'You like to drowned me.'

'Could still happen. Now where is he?'

'Jesus, you're a persistent cuss.'

'You want me to stop asking, tell me where he is.'

'At the house.' The man raised his arm and pointed up the mountain. 'Back at the house.'

Bodie had seen the man had no handgun. His rifle had been lost when Bodie hauled him out of his saddle and his knife was gone. He dragged the man out of the water and pushed him onto dry land. Bodie took out his own Colt and half-cocked the hammer so he could spin the cylinder, clearing water from the mechanism.

'Shells might be damp from all that water,' he said. 'She might not fire so take your chance if you feel lucky.'

The man glared up at the tall figure of the manhunter, checked the weapon, then the harsh expression on Bodie's face.

'What the hell you expecting me to do? Jump you?' he said. 'I may only be a simple mountain boy but I ain't that dumb.'

'Dumb enough to cover for Thad Monk.'

'He's kin. Family. That always come first.'

'He robbed a bank. Killed people.'

The man shrugged. 'Not the first time he done that.'

'What about shooting a woman? In the back. Some *kin* you got there.'

'You could be lyin',' the man said. He took a long moment. 'You after him for a bounty?'

'You figure I'd trail all this way just to deliver him a nosegay?'

'Thad's a mean son, but shootin' a woman . . . '

'He done it. Now I don't give a damn if you believe me or not. Get in my way and you'll be treated as hostile.'

'Damnit, mister, I *am* hostile. Whatever Thad's done he's still a Monk and that counts for somethin'.'

Bodie sighed. 'I knew you were going to say that.'

He half turned, leaving the man puzzled and off guard. Then he spun back and slammed the heavy Colt across the man's skull — twice. The man grunted and slumped over on his side, unconscious.

Bodie clawed his way back up the slope to where the man's horse stood, grazing on the damp grass. He picked up his rifle and saddlebags, grabbed at the horse's dangling reins and hauled himself into the saddle.

He hadn't forgotten there were still other members of the Monk clan around. Right there and then Bodie figured his best move was to back away, consider his options and plan his next move. His initial contact with Thad Monk's brethren had showed they were short on negotiating skills, but quick with dealing in lead. He was going to have to play them at their own game, but on his own terms.

13

Brand absorbed what he'd been told. Rankin and Calvin were prisoners of the Monks, and now so was he. The thought didn't sit right with him and he determined it wasn't going to stay that way for long. One way or another he had to break them all out. If the Monks stood in his way that would be their loss.

Rankin watched him close. The Marshal, despite his condition, had caught on to Brand's considered silence.

'You don't figure to stay too long,' he said.

Brand caught his eye. 'Like I said, I never been one to take being pushed around.'

'You've seen what they're like,' Calvin said. 'They won't tolerate any resistance.' He indicated the bruises on his face. 'How do you think we got like this . . . and we've seen bones in the mine workings. They don't hesitate to kill if they don't get their way.'

'He's right,' Rankin said. 'Hard bunch. Every last one of them. Killing would come easy to them. Look, Brand, I walked into this and they took me before I knew what was happening. I ain't proud of that. But give me a chance and I'll do my best to back any play you make.'

'Hell, Rankin, I got no call to belittle you. I didn't exactly come out too well myself. So next time we don't follow the book. They set the rules so we play by them.'

Brand checked out the room. It was solidly built. The only way out was through the single door.

'You showing up has changed their routine,' Rankin said. 'By now we'd be on our way to the mine.'

'They feed you first?'

Calvin nodded. 'Food's no problem. They know if they starve us we won't be able to work. So they bring us good meals.'

'How does that work?' Brand said.

'One of the women brings it on a tray. Armed man follows her in. Keeps her and us covered. Follows her out and locks the door again. Same happens when they come to collect the empties.'

'I saw the females when they brought me inside,' Brand said. 'Couple of them. Only saw them as I walked through. They didn't look too happy.'

'I got that feeling myself,' Rankin said.

'Maybe they're prisoners same as we are,' Calvin said. 'Could be they'd help us.'

'Right now I wouldn't count on that,' Brand said. 'We're not going to get much chance to ask them. Whatever we do we only have ourselves.'

'Look,' Calvin said, 'I've never been in anything like this before. Never owned a gun. Or used one.'

Rankin slapped him on the shoulder. 'Joseph, I doubt you ever used a pick

126

and shovel before you came here. Look at you now. Swings a pick like an expert.'

'What he's saying is when it matters a man can turn his hand to all kind of things,' Brand said. 'And if your own life depends on it you'll be surprised what you can turn your hand to.'

'Let's hope so,' Calvin said.

'Next time they come,' Brand said. 'No point putting it off.'

It was a long time coming. And some time later they heard gunshots. Then silence fell again. There was nothing they could do but wait. Beyond the window they heard thunder rumble and the rain sluice down.

For want of something to do Brand tugged up his right pants leg and slipped his fingers down inside his high boot, working out the six-inch bladed, slim knife he carried in a sheath sewn inside the boot. The razor sharp blade was topped by a handle of thin, tightly bound rough cord. It allowed for good purchase. He adjusted the pants leg again and slid the knife up his sleeve, readily available if the opportunity arose.

'They might regret missing that,' Rankin said.

Brand nodded. 'That's what I'm hoping. Just be ready to follow my lead if the chance shows.'

They waited again. Until the bolt on the door was slid back. As the door was pushed open one of the women Brand had seen earlier walked inside the room, carrying a large wooden tray.

She was in her early twenties, a slim girl, pretty rather than beautiful, with a face that would have been pleasant if she smiled. Her blonde hair, cut short, was unruly, framing her pale features and the bruises that marked her face. Fresh marks overlaid others that had been there longer. As she walked into the room her gaze fell on Brand, her blue eyes regarding him with a listless stare. The simple dress she wore looked as if it hadn't been washed for months and her feet were bare. She crossed the room and crouched to place the tray on the floor, then stood upright.

While this happened an armed man stood just inside the door, watching what happened. He carried a rifle in his hands and wore a heavy handgun strapped around his lean waist. His dark eyes took in everything.

'Get a move on, girl,' he said. 'You waste my time you'll be sorry.' He stared at the three prisoners. 'You got a half hour to eat.'

The girl's glance briefly lingered on Brand. Then she turned and walked out of the room. The door was swung shut, the bolt slammed home.

'Don't you just love their hospitality,' Rankin said.

On the tray were three deep tin plates holding a steaming meat stew. There were three tin cups of black coffee. No forks or spoons. The food had to be scooped out using their fingers.

'I believe they must have a damned barrel of this stew,' Calvin said between mouthfuls. 'Same thing every time.'

They devoured the food. Drank the bitter, gritty coffee.

Then they waited for the girl to come back.

The bolt snapped back, the door was dragged open and the girl walked in, her escort close behind this time. Brand saw the man was restless. He looked back over his shoulder, his gaze centered on the main room behind him. Brand recalled the shots they had heard. Something had happened and it was distracting the man.

Rankin and Calvin were squatting at the base of the wall again. Brand was on his feet, leaning against the wall across from the door, his arms held loosely together. He watched the young woman as she made her way to where the tray rested on the dirt floor. Her eyes settled on Brand for a few seconds as she stepped alongside him. He made no other move than to slightly incline his head, his eyes resting on hers.

She crouched to pick up the tray, lifted it, then let one side drop from her fingers. The plates rattled and one of the empty tin cups rolled onto the floor.

'Let me get that for you,' Brand said, pushing away from the wall and bending to scoop up the cup.

'*Hey,*' the man said, stepping forward to rap the barrel of his rifle across the girl's shoulder. 'Warned you not to go against me. I can pull this trigger sooner than waste my damn time with you. You know what happened to the others.'

His agitation forced his attention to waver between the girl and Brand as he roughly pushed her aside . . .

. . . and that was when Brand let the knife slip from under his sleeve. It dropped across his palm, stopped as his fingers curled around the cord grip. As Brand twisted his lowered body around he began to straighten and his eyes reached the level of the jailor's. In that brief connection the man recognized something in Brand's expression. When he registered the unflinching, cold stare he opened his mouth to yell a warning.

He was a lifetime too slow. Brand's left hand clamped across his mouth, pushing his head back. The slim blade in Brand's hand winked dully, then it sank into the man's exposed throat, going in deep, Brand sawing it back and forth. He heard the girl gasp. The ragged wound pulsed hot blood and the man began to choke. He let go of the rifle and Brand caught it in his left hand, tossing the weapon to Rankin as the Marshal pushed to his feet. Brand snatched the holstered Colt free and pulled back the hammer as the choking man sagged to his knees, both hands going to the wound in his throat, his fingers turning red from the bubbling flow.

'*Move, girl*,' Brand said as he slid the knife back in its boot sheath.

She gathered herself, tearing her gaze from the bloodied figure and scuttled across the floor to press up against the wall, next to Calvin. He was staring, eyes wide, taking in the spectacle of the dying man on the floor.

'Cover me, Rankin,' Brand snapped, moving forward to clear the door as he ducked through into the main room beyond.

Hec Rankin stepped up to the open doorway, staring out into the large communal room.

Already clear of the doorway Brand scanned the room. Across the far side a figure was already turning, sharp, feral eyes seeking movement. A lean, shaggy-haired figure in homespun clothing, wielding a long-barreled Walker Colt. The man — more of a youngster — laid his gaze on Brand. Realized who he was and snapped up the heavy revolver. The muzzle spat flame and smoke. Brand felt the wind of the slug's passing before it chunked into the solid frame of the door inches to one side of his body. The shooter uttered a low curse, hauling back on the hammer for a second shot — which he never made — as Brand triggered his own weapon. The Colt in his hand had settled on target and the

133

heavy .45 slug slammed into the man's skinny chest. He fell back with a screech, flesh cleaved and bone splintered by the slug.

Rankin turned about and gestured at Calvin and the girl.

'Let's get out of here,' he said.

The girl pushed to her feet and crossed the room. Calvin hung back, eyes still fixed on the bloody figure on the floor.

'Calvin, let's go before anyone comes back,' Rankin said.

Brand caught hold of the girl's arm, pulling her close.

'Stay with me,' he said.

She nodded. 'I will.'

The main door crashed open and an armed figure stood in the opening, taking in the scene. He spotted Brand and the girl. The long-barreled Henry repeating rifle he carried swung up and the man pulled the trigger, sending a slug across the room. It plowed into the wall behind Brand. He returned fire, his slug taking the man in the left shoulder.

A second later the rifle Rankin held sent out a pair of 44–40 slugs. They drove the man to the floor.

'There a back way out of here?' Brand asked.

'This way,' the girl said, tugging his sleeve.

She led them to the side, through an open doorway into the kitchen area. A wood-burning stove and oven dominated one wall, with a heavy wooden table in the center of the room. The other woman Brand had seen earlier was standing beside the table, a dazed expression on her face. She was older than the girl at Brand's side, her body heavy under the ragged gray dress.

'Hannah, let's get out of here,' the girl said.

The older woman shook her head. 'We can't,' she said. 'He won't like us running off. He'll beat us again . . . '

Brand pulled the girl with him. He could see the fear on the older woman's eyes. Whatever had been done to her in this place had left her too scared to back away.

'Hell, Brand, we don't have time to talk this over,' Rankin said as he came up behind, dragging Calvin by his sleeve. 'I got enough problems with Calvin here.'

'What's your name?' Brand asked the girl at his side.

'Joanne.'

'Joanne, you've got ten seconds to get her to move, and that may be time we don't have.'

Joanne turned to the woman and caught her hands, tugging her forward.

'Hannah, come along. If we stay they'll come and get us.'

The older woman stared at her, face white with fear. 'I can't go. I'll hold you up. Just leave. Save yourself.'

She wrenched her hands free and backed away, then made a desperate run across the room in the direction of the main door.

And as she reached it she began to scream.

'*In here. They're in here.*'

'That's all we need,' Brand said. 'We have to go. *Now.*'

The girl took a last look at Hannah, then fell in beside Brand as they made for the door at the far side of the kitchen. Rankin had jerked the wooden door open, pushing Calvin through. Brand followed the lawman out through the door, Joanne close at his side.

The rain had ceased falling and the heavy cloud had drifted away.

A gun fired from across the room, the slug tearing a chunk of wood out of the door frame.

Brand didn't look back.

He didn't need to — he knew the Monks wouldn't be far behind.

'Head for the trees,' Brand yelled.

They were crossing the back yard of the house. Through puddled water and soft ground. A cluttered area of stacked timber and barrels. Long-accumulated junk. Beyond the yard the ground fell away in an uneven slope. Chickens squawked and fled away from them as

137

Rankin led the way to the timber some two hundred and fifty yards away. Brand wasn't too happy at having to cross the relatively open ground but they had no choice. Their first priority was to reach cover away from the guns of the Monks.

14

Rankin and Calvin led the way, with Joanne behind them. Brand brought up the rear, watching their back trail. He was expecting the Monks to show up at any minute.

His expectations were resolved moments later.

The drum of hoofs reached him.

Brand turned and saw a mounted and armed man coming at them from around the front of the house. Hunched over the neck of his horse, the man had a gun in his free hand, aimed in their direction. The revolver fired. The slug kicking up dirt yards away.

That was when Joanne missed her stride and went to her knees.

Brand reached her, standing over her exposed body, his revolver picking up the advancing rider. He held himself motionless as he gripped the Colt two-handed, seeing the rider and horse grow larger. The rider leaned out from behind the horse's neck, lowering his gun hand and settling his aim.

Brand's finger eased back the trigger. He felt the revolver buck in his grasp. Heard the slam of the shot. Saw a flash of red as the .45 slug ripped into the rider's chest, high up and on the left. The rider's cry was lost in the thunder of the pounding hoofs as he went backwards out of the saddle. The man rolled over the horse's flanks and slammed face down on the ground with a heavy thump. The riderless horse kept coming and Brand held up both hands as it closed in. At the last moment the animal balked, coming to a noisy stop. Brand snatched at the dangling reins, hauling it round. He pulled the animal close, keeping it between himself and the house.

'*On your feet,*' he yelled to Joanne.

She stood and instinctively moved beside him and fell into step as she kept moving. Her hand reached out to grasp the dangling stirrup.

Brand had already spotted the rifle jammed into the sheath. He holstered the Colt and used his right hand to pull the rifle from the scabbard.

Up ahead Rankin and Calvin reached the cover of the timber.

The crack of a rifle from the direction of the house was followed by the slug slamming into a tree trunk that sent bark and wood slivers flying.

Brand tugged on the reins, leading the horse into cover. He passed the reins to Joanne and she pulled the animal deeper into the protection of the timber.

'Close,' Rankin said as they pushed deeper into the timber.

'We need to gain some distance,' Brand said. 'They're going to get themselves organized and come after us.'

They kept moving. The daylight reduced by the overhead canopy of intertwined tree branches and leaves. Brand pushed them on for the next half hour before he called a brief halt.

He opened the saddlebags strapped to the rear of the horse and went through the contents. A couple of shirts. A roll of oilskin holding a number of matches and a bundle of rough cigars. He also found a second revolver and a leather pouch heavy with ammunition. When he opened the pouch he found it held a mix of .45 and .44–40 shells. While Rankin kept watch Brand loaded all their weapons. Now they had a pair of handguns and two rifles. There was a jug of liquor dangling from the saddle horn by a rawhide thong.

'Take this,' Brand said, holding out one of the revolvers in Calvin's direction.

The man shook his head. 'I wouldn't know what to do with it,' he said.

'I would.'

Brand glanced at Joanne. The determined look in her eyes told him she wasn't fooling. He handed her the Colt, watched as she checked it with sure actions. The heavy weapon looked large in her slim hand.

'Don't worry about me, Brand. One thing I can tell you right now. There's no way I'm going back there. The Monks took me from my family after they killed them. Made me a prisoner in that house. I'm going to stay alive so I can pay them back if I get the chance.' The determined look on her face made Brand believe her. 'You believe vengeance is a right only men can have? Well, not this time.'

'Calvin, you stay with her,' Brand said. 'Real close.'

The geologist simply nodded.

'You got a plan?' Rankin asked.

'Plain and simple. We get the hell down off this damned mountain.'

Joanne said, 'The Monks are spread across the area. A couple more homesteads to the north and west. Most of them kin. They can send for help if they need it.'

'Not the news I was hoping for.'

'I just wanted you to know what we're up against.'

Rankin said, 'Riders comin'.'

'Joanne, take the saddle,' Brand said. 'You get up behind her, Calvin. Let's move out. Rankin, you stay close to that horse. Just keep them moving away from here.'

'You staying back?'

'Just long enough to suggest they don't follow.'

He braced himself behind a thick trunk as his group moved deeper into the timber, bringing the rifle to his shoulder. The three riders were close enough to be well in range. Brand brought the lead rider into focus, finger curling against the trigger. He could have killed the man easily but chose instead to put the .44–40 lead slug into the man's shoulder. Time enough for killing if the Monks kept pushing too hard. The rider jerked to one side as the slug ripped in through the fleshy part of his shoulder. A flash of red showed as it exited. The rider reared back, dropping his rifle as he slewed out of his saddle and hit the ground in a cursing heap.

The other riders hauled in on their reins, leveled their own weapons and sent a ragged volley of shots in Brand's direction. He had already dropped to a crouch and heard the slugs chunk into tree trunks and whip through the foliage. He brought up his rifle again and returned fire, levering over and over, laying down a burst of shots that scattered the riders, one catching a slug in his right leg.

Struggling to contain the panicky horses, the riders forgot about pursuit as they hauled on their reins. The leg-shot man hung on to his saddle, blood soaking his pants where Brand's slug had torn the flesh. The third man, untouched, slid from his saddle to help the shoulder-shot man. Brand was forgotten as they moved back, simply intent to save themselves.

Brand turned and pushed deeper into the stand of timber. He could make out the others ahead of him, Rankin making sure Joanne kept the horse moving.

For the moment, Brand decided, they had a reprieve. He didn't expect it to last for long. Sooner or later the Monks were going to regroup and take up the pursuit again, and they would be a damn sight more cautious next time.

It was far from over.

15

Bodie knew he allowed his recklessness to get the better of him at times. He let himself be led by the feelings of the moment rather than by taking time to consider what he was letting himself in for. Even so he knew that this time around, whatever the outcome, he was not riding away. Almost from the moment he had taken out after Thad Monk he had been shot at, lost his horse and generally had a run of bad luck. All of which totaled up to leave him a tad upset.

Anyone who knew him would realize that unsettling Bodie was not something to be considered. In this case the Monk clan did *not* know Bodie. But they were going to and any that survived would be able to sit back and realize the error of their ways.

As he pushed his borrowed horse

back towards the Monk spread Bodie took time to work on the situation. He had no idea what had caused the outbreak of gunfire he had heard. There would easily be a number of explanations. When he thought about them he couldn't see any that might be of benefit to himself. The last thing he needed was to get himself caught up in some dispute not of his own making.

He acknowledged the shooting might have been from some other lawful group come up the mountain to deal with the Monk clan. They were no bunch of peace lovers, more along the lines of a reclusive clan of mountain dwellers who expected to be left alone and who protected their own and who would not welcome strangers. Something not unheard of when it came to these mountain dwellers. The possibilities were numerous. All he wanted was to get his hands on Thad Monk so he could haul him, dead or alive, back to collect the bounty.

There were times, he decided, when

a man had to deal with all kinds of distractions just to earn himself an honest dollar. This was one of them. It seemed Bodie was going to have to wade through more than his fair share of them before he got his hands on Thaddeus Monk.

He pushed on, telling himself he would come through this damn mess in the end. He'd been riding the bounty trail for too long to allow a few setbacks to make him quit. In truth Bodie never did quit. It wasn't in his nature to give in just because things became rough.

Bodie let his thoughts take him back to the previous encounter with the Monk clan when he had approached the house. If he was going to revisit the place he needed to go in with less of a fanfare, using some stealth, and to that end he decided he would ride around the place and come in from a less than direct point. He reined the horse west, figuring to make a wide approach and tackle the homestead from the far side. It would mean a longer ride but

Bodie never concerned himself with time limits. Better to make a slower approach than catch a fast bullet.

He felt the hot sun on him as he rode. A shade more comfortable than the sudden rain storm of the previous day. The horse had no quarrel with the slow pace of travel. The day had taken on a quieter aspect and Bodie was never one to argue with that. His man-hunting life had a habit of becoming dark and violent when things were on the move and right now was no exception.

16

Adam's clothes still felt damp from the rain storm. He had managed to find himself some cover but not before the deluge soaked him through. He had spent long hours through the night sitting in front of the small fire he had built. It threw out some heat, though not enough to dry him out and he called himself every kind of a fool for not making sure he had a slicker tied behind his saddle. Despite his condition he'd had to smile when he imagined what his pa would have said to such a fool mistake.

His father.

He was still coming to terms with the fact. He had found him, but Brand had ridden out so quickly they hadn't really had time to forge any kind of bond. Adam hadn't expected it to happen instantly. He just wanted to get to know the man. Which was why he had acted on impulse, hiring the horse and following his father up into the hills. He knew Brand would be mad as hell when he showed up and the boy admitted what he'd done was downright foolish.

At least he had brought his rifle along with him. Coming all this way without a means to protect himself would have been even more foolish than actually striking out on his own. He had heard distant gunfire and he couldn't help wondering if his father had been involved. Adam didn't dwell on that for too long. He held the feeling Brand was well able to take care of himself. With those thoughts on his mind he pushed on across the timbered slopes, admitting to himself he was having some problems tracking. The rain had washed out most of the tracks he had been following and he had to cast around, retrace his steps while he kept up his search.

He found tracks finally but they comprised more than one horse. And the way they were spread out, meandering back and forth, told him they were searching for something, cutting about in a haphazard way. What were the searchers looking for? More likely *who* were they looking for.

His father's image came into his mind.

Was he the subject of the search?

Adam took to his saddle, worry in his mind now. He needed to find his father. To find him unhurt and alive.

He told himself he had been right to go searching for Brand. If his father was in possible danger he wanted to be around. To help if he could.

Mid-morning and the rain that had swept the mountain slopes had gone. The sun was back in a cloudless sky, the heat pressing down through the trees. Adam rode with a sense of urgency behind his actions now.

Where was his father?

Sporadic gunfire came and went. Echoes rattled across the slopes, distorted by the clustered timber and he found it hard to pinpoint where exactly the shots came from. He admitted to himself that his tracking skills were not as good as he might have imagined. Becoming an expert took years of dedication. More time than he had spent.

He spotted the gleam of water, decided to stop to refill his canteen. He pulled his horse towards the rushing stream that originated somewhere far higher up the mountain. His horse picked up the scent and turned sharply. Adam's lack of concentration left him unprepared for the animal's unexpected move. He felt himself sliding sideways from the saddle, lost his grip on the reins and pitched off the horse. He landed awkwardly, thrown forward across the slope above the stream. When he landed he lost his balance and smacked down on his stomach, throwing out his hands to halt his fall. The impact punched the air out of his lungs a second before he bounced his head against a half-buried rock. The blow was hard enough to open a gash above his right eye that bled heavily as Adam stretched out motionless in the lush grass.

And sometime later that was where Bodie found him.

17

They took a break after an hour of steady travel, still deep in timbered country. Rankin had spotted a shallow stream foaming down from a higher level and the four of them welcomed the sight of the water. They took it in turns to drink and splash the cool water on their faces.

'I never thought water could taste so nice,' Joanne said.

Rankin had unhooked the canteen hanging on the saddle. He poured out the contents, rinsed out the canteen and refilled it with fresh water.

Brand had taken up a position where he could watch their back trail. They might not have seen any signs of pursuit but he was taking no chances. The way things had unfolded he wasn't about to let his guard down.

'They're out there alright,' Rankin

said. 'No way they're going to just forget about us.'

'They have too much to hide,' Brand said. 'The mine. The killings. And we've hurt them.'

'These mountain boys close ranks when something threatens them. And they know these hills. It's their backyard and they'll do everything they can to protect it.'

'We'll rest for a while,' Brand said. 'Just stay close. No wandering off.'

'You think any of us is going to do that?' Calvin said peevishly. 'This is not what I was supposed to be involved with.'

He was slumped against a fallen log and stared at Brand as if he was responsible for everything that had happened. The man was not taking their position well. Brand was beginning to lose patience with him. He couldn't help comparing Calvin's self-pity to the way Joanne was handling things. The young woman was holding up strongly, her stubborn nature adding to her strength. Her spirit would see her through whatever problems they might face.

'Face it, Calvin. This is how things are. None of us want it but the Monks aren't about to let us go without a fight,' Brand said.

'Then it's down to you and Rankin,' Calvin snapped back. 'Isn't that what you're paid to do? Protect us.'

Rankin turned, his face angry. He stood over Calvin, hands gripping his rifle. His shoulders were set, tension visible in every part of him.

'Calvin, I've heard enough from you. Mister, this isn't just your problem. We're in this together and you better realize that. I heard enough of your whining. None of us chose for this to happen — but it has. You take a long look at this lady, here, and quit acting like a spoiled brat. She's showing more backbone than you'll ever have.'

Joanne glanced at the Marshal, color rising in her cheeks.

The sudden eruption of roosting

birds from the undergrowth behind them caught Brand's attention. He didn't hesitate. The flight meant only one thing.

'Down,' he called. '*Get down.*'

A barrage of shots blasted sound over his yell. Rifle fire. From more than one weapon.

Brand lunged at Joanne, slamming into her and brought her to the ground.

Out the corner of his eye he saw Rankin fall back, a rifle slug tearing into his left shoulder. The lawman dropped to the ground, his rifle lost from his grip.

The shooting continued and Calvin was caught as he rose to his feet in panic. A half dozen rifle slugs struck him, tearing bloody holes in his side and back. A final shot took away one side of his face and he pitched down on the ground.

Covering Joanne with his prone body Brand swung his rifle around and returned fire in the direction the shots came from. He had seen the muzzle flash from the weapons and triggered the magazine's load as fast as he could work the rifle. When it clicked empty he pulled the Colt from his holster and used that.

'*Brand.*'

He heard Rankin's strained voice, turned and saw the Marshal pushing his own rifle in Brand's direction. He snatched it up, sheathed the Colt and laid down more fire at the ambush site. He had used up half the magazine when he realized there was no more return fire. He slid off Joanne. Stayed low to the ground as he eyed the ambush site.

' . . . *nearly suffocated me,*' he heard the woman say.

Still able to make her presence felt, he realized.

'Better than a bullet,' he said.

'Have they gone?' she asked.

Brand pushed her back down as he started to rise.

'More than likely not. Let's find out before we raise any flags.'

'I can't see any movement back there,' Rankin said. 'Either they've backed off, or you put them down.'

'Stay down,' Brand said. 'I need to circle around and come up behind them.'

As he spoke he was thumbing fresh loads into the Colt from his belt loops.

'Be careful,' Joanne said.

Crouching, Brand angled for cover, slipping in between thick tree trunks, starting to circle around the ambush position. He moved as fast as he could without creating too much noise. He was aware that the hidden men might be waiting for him to show himself. It was a risk he was willing to take. He had no idea how many he might be facing, or whether there were others close by. If there were the gunfire might bring them on the run.

He took himself well to the rear of the shooters' position, using the timber and the tangled undergrowth as cover. He kept the spot he was approaching in his sights, searching for any movement that might tell him what he could be facing. The intensity of the recent shooting suggested there was more than one of them and he had to consider they might still be alive and able to shoot back.

Brand felt sweat finger its way down the side of his face. In amongst the greenery the day's heat remained trapped and it was getting uncomfortable. His shirt was sticking to his back. Brand flicked at the moisture threatening to sting his eyes.

He froze as he caught a shadow ahead, still part-hidden by the undergrowth. Something dark. Like clothing. A man's shirt. Brand focused on the spot, peering through the greenery. It was definitely clothing. He saw the shape move. Picked up a low, hesitant voice as someone spoke.

Brand raised the rifle, feeling the weapon slippery in his grasp. He wiped each hand on his pants in turn.

The voice he had heard came again and Brand realized the man was muttering to himself rather than conversing with someone else.

Brand thought about Rankin and Calvin. The amount of times the geologist had been hit Brand doubted he was still alive. The lawman had been hit in the shoulder and would need seeing to. Time was wasting. He stepped to the side, closing in on the ambush site and pushed through the undergrowth, coming up behind the concealed shooters.

And found one man on his back, bullet holes in his chest.

A second man crouched against the trunk of a tree, rifle on the ground at his feet. He was the one talking . . . mumbling more to himself than anyone who might be listening. He raised his head when Brand appeared. He was bleeding from the mouth. There was more blood coming from the holes in his body, his hands clasped there in an attempt to stop the heavy flow. He stared up at Brand, his eyes focusing.

'You done for us,' he said. 'Shot us to pieces.'

'No more'n you asked for.'

'Nathaniel, he's goin' to hunt you down . . . '

'He'll need to make a better showing than you boys.'

A slow cough bubbled up from the man's chest. He dribbled more blood from his slack mouth. He folded forward, body hunching over. His breathing was labored, becoming less.

Brand backed off. There was no more to fear from the pair. He walked out into the open and made his way back to where Joanne was bending over Rankin, doing what she could for his wound. She looked up at him. Her hands were red with Rankin's blood.

'Calvin didn't make it,' she said quietly.

'I figured that.'

She waved a hand in the general direction of the way they had come.

'Are *they* dead?'

'One is,' Brand said. 'Other one is

well on his way to catching up.'

'Did they have horses?' Joanne asked. 'We could use them.'

'Didn't see them close by. Wasn't worth the risk looking for them if there are others around.' Brand checked out Rankin. 'That slug caught you hard.'

'Almost worth getting shot to have her tending me,' the lawman said. His voice was low and breathy.

'Trouble is I can't do much more,' Joanne said.

She had torn a couple of cloth strips from her dress to press over the puckered bullet hole in Rankin's shoulder.

'You're doing fine. Just stay with him.'

Brand walked to where their horse was standing yards away. It turned its head and moved nervously as he got near. Brand held out a reassuring hand, talking quietly to the animal until he was able to take hold of the dangling reins. He ran a hand along its neck to calm it, then gently led it back to Joanne and Rankin. He wrapped the reins around a low branch, went to the saddlebags and took one of the shirts. He handed it to Joanne. He passed her the knife from his boot sheath so she could fashion crude bandages to wrap around Rankin's shoulder.

'Best I can do,' she said.

She rubbed her bloodied hands down her dress. She took the canteen Brand unhooked from the saddle and gave Rankin a taste of water.

'Any liquor in those saddlebags?' the Marshal asked.

'A jug of homemade liquor hanging from the saddle.'

Brand brought it and Joanne pulled the stopper. Gave Rankin a drink.

'That is vicious stuff,' the lawman said. His face puckered as he spoke. 'But what the hell.'

Joanna allowed him a second swallow before she handed the jug to Brand to hang back from the saddle.

Brand reloaded the rifles and hand-guns from the ammunition pouch. He jammed one into the empty scabbard on the horse. He took a swallow from the canteen.

'Not going to taste that liquor?' Rankin said.

'I need a clear head,' Brand said.

'What now?' Joanne asked.

'We get ourselves as far away from the Monks as we can,' Brand said. 'Certain sure they haven't upped and quit on us.'

Joanne took him aside.

'We need to get Hec somewhere safe. That bullet needs to come out before too long.'

Brand knew she was talking sense. The longer the piece of lead stayed in Rankin's wound the more likely complications could set in.

A bullet wound brought with it more than simply injury to flesh. Infection. Dirt drawn into the wound as it entered could cause that. They could do without complications.

'I know what you're saying. Not so easy to do stuck out here in the middle of nowhere.'

'Jason, we have to do *something* for him.'

Brand couldn't argue with that.

'Hec, we need to move on. Find ourselves a place we can deal with that wound. Sooner than later.'

Brand bent over Rankin and raised him off the ground. He heard the man groan softly. Ignored it. Moving Rankin was going to hurt him but it had to be done.

'Keep the horse steady,' Brand said.

Joanne took the reins, stroked the horse's head. She watched as Brand boosted Rankin into the saddle.

'You'll need to get up behind and hold him steady.'

She passed the Colt she was holding to Brand. With his help she pulled herself onto the horse, gripping Rankin. Brand returned the revolver to her, took the reins and without a word led the horse forward.

'What about Calvin?'

'I understand what you mean but there's nothing we can do for him now,'

Brand told her. 'He's dead. We're not and if we want to stay that way we need to move.'

Joanne might have protested if he hadn't been right. It didn't sit too well having to leave Calvin's body where it was but their needs were greater. Rankin's need was to stay in the saddle. His wound was not doing him any favors. His pain refused to let up and with every step the horse took Joanne felt the man shudder. All she could do was hang onto him and try to keep him from slipping out of the saddle.

'Jason,' she said. He glanced up at her and she added, 'Over to the west I recall there being an old mine settlement. Been abandoned for years but there might be a place we can use. At least it'll offer some cover while we do what we can for Hec's shoulder.'

'Worth looking at.'

He followed her instructions and in less than an hour they came on the deserted cluster of buildings. A half dozen wooden structures, all in various states of decay, with weeds and brush growing around them. Given time the mountain would reclaim the land and absorb the huts.

★ ★ ★

By this time Rankin was more unconscious than awake and Joanne was struggling to keep him upright. She made no complaints. Simply held his body close and chose to ignore the sticky feel of blood that had leaked from the shoulder wound.

Brand brought them to the soundest of the shacks, which wasn't saying a great deal when he checked its condition. He led the horse up close and looped the reins around a loose timber.

'Help him,' Joanne said.

'Bring the saddlebags and blanket roll,' Brand said as he eased the lawman down off the horse and found he needed to support the weakened man. Ahead of him Joanne had pushed open the door, stepping inside, and Brand followed. By this time he was practically carrying Rankin.

The interior was filled with a scattering of furniture. A few wooden benches and chairs. A solid wood table set in the center of the room.

Brand swept the table top clear and eased Rankin onto it. He slid his knife from the boot sheath and handed it to Joanne.

'Cut away his shirt so we can see the bullet hole.'

While she did that he stepped back outside and took the rifle from the scabbard. He brought the jug of liquor with him.

'Do you think they'll find us?' Joanne asked.

'It's their territory. Let's hope they're still of a mind we'll keep moving on.'

He stood over Rankin, examining the wound. He could see where the slug had gone in, close to the shoulder bone. The flesh around and above the wound was discolored, still weeping blood.

'What are you thinking?' Joanne asked.

'Bullet's close to the bone. Must be giving him a lot of pain.'

'He's a brave man.'

'And he might end up being a dead man if we can't get that slug out.'

'Not much of a choice then,' Joanne said.

'We cut out that slug it's going to make a mess. No guarantee the shock might not kill him.'

'You have to try.'

Brand opened the saddlebag and pulled out the other shirt he'd seen earlier. He cut it into a number of strips. He doused the blade of his knife with liquor from the jar and wiped it with a piece of shirt cloth, then poured more onto his hands and cleaned them as best he could. He soaked a wadded fold of material and handed it to Joanne.

'How will you do it?' she asked.

'I'm no doctor. All I can do is cut around the hole. Make it bigger so I can see the slug and try to dig it out.'

'But won't that . . . ?'

Brand glanced at her. 'Hurt him like hell? Yeah.'

'*Damnit, I'm still here*,' Rankin muttered, his voice rough and barely audible. 'Just do it . . . and give me some more of that liquor.'

Brand handed the jug over. Joanne raised Rankin's head as he put the jug to his lips. He drank long and hard, gasping as the fiery liquid slid down his throat.

'Jesus, that stuff is still evil.'

Brand stood over the lawman, catching Joanne's nervous gaze. She didn't say anything, simply gave him a slight nod.

'Be ready with that cloth,' he said.

Brand gripped the knife. *This is foolishness*, he told himself. *I'm no damn doctor.* With that thought in mind he pressed his left hand over the bullet wound, then made a quick incision that cut in deep. Blood immediately bubbled from the cut.

Without needing to be told Joanne wiped it away with her cloth. Rankin had let out a low moan, his body arching up off the table. Brand leaned down hard with his left hand, already red with blood, and held the man as still as he could. There was no easy way to do this. Rankin was going to have to take the pain and to give him his due the man held himself as still as he was able. Brand spread the wound with his fingers, trying to see the bullet. The incision had exposed pinkish inner flesh and when Brand probed with the tip of the knife, easing it in deeper, he felt something hard grate against the blade. Rankin's body shuddered and a low, continuous moan came from him. Brand felt sweat pop out across his face. He shook blood from his hands and bent over the wound again. This time as the steel blade moved against the piece of embedded lead Rankin let out a hard gasp, his body twisting in agony. The blade moved, slicing into the flesh.

'Oh hell,' Rankin yelled, twisting violently.

'*Damnit*,' Brand said.

He transferred the knife to his left hand, bunched his fist and punched Rankin hard across his jaw. The blow snapped the lawman's head to one side, the force rendering him unconscious.

Brand heard Joanne gasp. Her face was colorless, eyes wide with surprise.

'You have a better solution?' he snapped.

'Not really,' she said. She cradled Rankin's head against her and swabbed the bleeding wound again.

With Rankin's resistance stopped Brand bent to his task again and this time he forced himself to complete it. He worked the tip of the blade beneath the bullet and tried to ease it out. The lead slug was held tight by flesh and muscle. More blood pulsed from around the bullet. Brand put the knife aside and pushed finger and thumb deep into the cavity. He forced his way around the bullet, his grip hampered by the blood slick.

'*God damn it. Come out you sonofa-bitch.*'

'Does all that cursing actually do any good?' Joanne asked.

'Right now it does it for me.'

Without warning the bullet moved. Brand sucked in a breath and held it. He worked the resistant lead, fraction by fraction, until it came free with a wet sound. He raised his hand and showed the bullet to Joanne. She acknowledged him with a slight nod, then tipped liquor from the jug into the open wound and wiped it with a fresh wad of cloth. Brand sluiced his bloodied hands with water from the canteen, then helped her press a fold of liquor-soaked cloth over the wound. Between them they bound the shoulder with more strips of cloth, pulling it as tight as they could. Blood quickly showed through the bandage but there was nothing they could do about that. When they draped one of the blankets from the bed roll over Rankin he was beginning to stir restlessly.

'If he survives,' Joanne said, 'it will be thanks to you.' She put a hand on his arm. 'Thank you, Jason.'

'I just hope I haven't made things worse for him.'

'Hell, no, I'm feeling better already.' Rankin was staring up at them, his bloodless face sheened with sweat. He raised his free hand and rubbed his bruised jaw. 'That was a hell of a wallop you put me out with, *hombre*.'

'All I could think of at the time.' Brand held out the slug he was holding. 'Damn thing put up a hell of a fight.'

'I need a drink,' Rankin husked.

Joanne put the jug to his lips again and Rankin took a swallow.

'Still evil-tasting,' he said.

Brand took the jug from Joanne and took a swallow himself. He felt the fiery brew burn its way down to his stomach.

'Got to agree with you. That is real homemade evil.'

Joanne cleaned her own hands. She took a turn around the room, peering into corners to distract herself from what she had witnessed.

'Brand, I owe you,' Rankin said.

'Thank me when you're on your feet again.'

'I can feel you want to be on the move.'

'The Monks aren't going to stop looking for us,' Brand reminded him.

'And I'm holding you back.' Rankin's face registered the pain he was still feeling. 'Maybe you should go. Leave me a gun and get the hell out of here.'

'No.'

Joanne's protest was strong. She moved back to stand next to the table, placing a hand on Rankin.

'We have to stay together,' she said.

'If we leave we'll be an easy target for them,' Rankin said.

'So we're caught whichever way we choose,' Brand said. 'If it's down to me I'd rather we were in the open, not trapped in here. If the Monks find us all they have to do is wait us out. Or burn us out.'

'Which is why we need to leave,' Rankin added.

'What do you think?' Joanne asked Brand.

'Hec's got a point. They catch us in here our chances are poor. At least outside we have a chance to stay ahead of them. Not great choices but we need to make one or the other.'

'Stay or go,' Joanne said, 'Hec needs to rest. A couple of hours at least. Move him now and that wound will just start to bleed again.'

'Few hours and it'll be dark,' Brand said. 'That could work for us. Make it harder for the Monks to follow.'

Rankin said, 'What are you thinking, Jason?'

'That I might take a look around. Before it gets dark. Pick out a way we can go that'll take us well away from the Monks.'

'Do it,' Rankin said. 'Leave us something to defend ourselves.'

Brand left them one of the rifles and a handgun.

'Just make sure you leave that jug,' Rankin said. 'I might need to fortify myself if things get tense.'

'You take care,' Joanne said as Brand opened the door and slipped out.

18

Brand rode with caution uppermost in his mind. He allowed the horse to make its own pace as he moved through the timber. He had positioned himself and it took him no real time to work out the best route for them. The unmarked trail meandered across ground that would lead them to the lower slopes.

He saw no one. Heard nothing apart from the natural sounds of the land. If the Monks were around they were staying quiet. Brand kept the rifle across his saddle, ready for use. Something told him he was pretty much alone on this section of the mountain. Brand didn't allow that to lessen his mood. Taking too much for granted could lead a man to lowering his defenses and that was one way to put himself at risk.

Sitting his horse Brand gazed out

across the open fall of the long slopes in front of him. A silent, sprawling vista of trees and an empty landscape that would take them back in the direction of Santa Fe. Brand studied the way and memorized the terrain so that even night travel would be reasonable. It might be the long way around but it presented them with the least problems — apart from the Monks if they showed their hand.

He decided it was time he made his way back to where Rankin and Joanne were waiting. They needed to be set on their way now. Brand turned his horse and rode back into the closeness of the timber, following his own tracks. He picked up the sound of running water close by and decided to take time to allow the horse to drink. Reining about Brand pushed through the close stand of timber shielding the water source. As he came clear he drew rein, fixing his gaze on the scene unfolding in front of him.

He took a moment to take in that

what he was seeing was real . . .

A pair of horses close by.

A big, tall, shaggy-haired man standing over a figure on the ground. Close enough to see the bright blood streaking the sprawled figure's face.

His son's face.

It was Adam . . .

Brand didn't waste time wondering why the boy was here. All that mattered was Adam's presence and the fact he was hurt, with someone standing over him . . .

Brand took it in at a glance and anger flooded his reasoning, pushing aside any other thoughts. All he could see was his son Adam, slumped on the ground with blood on his face.

And the towering figure standing over him, reaching down for the boy.

Brand drove his heels into his horse's side, sending it powering forward towards the two figures. He slipped his feet free from the stirrups and as the horse pounded in close Brand launched himself from the saddle, letting go of the rifle and pushing his arms out in front as he reached for the tall man . . .

* * *

. . . Bodie heard the rush of sound. Turned about and saw a equally tall, broad-shouldered figure throwing himself from the back of the hard-striding horse. There was no time to do anything but throw up his hands before the man slammed into him. Locked together Brand and Bodie crashed hard to the ground, breath bursting from their lungs as they hit. For seconds they were a struggling shape, each attempting to gain the advantage.

As they broke apart, pushing to their feet, Brand aimed a clenched fist that caught Bodie across his left cheek. The blow rocked the man hunter's head, shaggy hair flying as he registered the blow. His own big fist swept up and landed on Brand's shoulder, the force behind the blow pulling him up short. Bodie followed up fast, swinging his left fist round and caught Brand on his lower jaw. Brand recovered, planting his feet and lashing out with a punch that connected with Bodie's ribs, then stepped in close and took hold of Bodie's shirt, pulling him towards him. The move was smooth and Bodie had no chance to step away. Brand made a sudden, twisting move, hauling Bodie over his hip and Bodie felt himself being swept off his feet and through the air. He landed hard on his back and saw the other man moving in. Aches flaring in his bruised body Bodie, rolled on his side, coiling up one leg and kicking out. His booted foot caught Brand in his stomach, bending him forward. As Brand's head lowered Bodie pushed himself off the ground and swung a hard right as he rose to his knees. The punch caught Brand across the mouth. His head twisted, blood flying from torn lips. He sensed Bodie sliding in closer and forced himself to respond, spitting blood from his mouth and bringing up both hands to block the heavy blows coming at him. He took one to the chest, responding with a solid punch that clouted his opponent on his jaw, opening a cut that bled quickly. They traded blows, neither willing to give an inch, or quit, as they edged back and forth, taking and giving hits.

They would have battered each other senseless if Adam, recovering enough to realize what was happening, hadn't pushed his feet and stumbled awkwardly towards them.

'*Stop,*' he yelled.

Neither man paid any attention, still continued to throw punches, and they would have battered each other senseless if the boy hadn't pushed himself between them, his hands holding them apart.

'Listen to me. *Damn it, listen to me.*' He stared at Brand. 'He was helping me, pa.' He swung his head in Bodie's direction. 'This is my pa. He's my father. *My father.*'

Bodie's fist stopped in mid-air.

'*Sonofabitch*,' he said. 'That the truth, boy?'

Adam nodded. Swaying on his feet. Still weak from the fall.

Brand stepped back, backhanding blood from a gash over one eye. He was sucking air into his lungs. He stared at Bodie.

'I know you,' he said. 'Been a while since I saw you. You're Bodie? The one they call *The Stalker*?'

'I been called that. And other things.'

'You on a hunt now?'

'Yeah. I taken out after a feller called Thad Monk. He's wanted for robbery and murder. Killed a woman. Shot her in the back 'cause she got in his way. I was following when your boy, here, got himself in trouble when his horse threw him.'

Brand dropped his defensive posture, shaking his head at the mix-up.

'Seems I owe you.' He indicated the other's bloody face. 'Glad we chose fists and not guns.'

'You got that right.'

187

Brand glanced at Adam, who had chosen to remain silent.

'Now isn't the time, boy, but we need to have a talk later.'

'I couldn't just sit back in town,' Adam said. 'I had to find you, pa.'

'This is all very touching,' Bodie said, 'but right now we got other things to worry over. Like it or not, we've got a whole bunch of guns searching these mountains for us.' He paused and eyed Brand. 'Damned if I just didn't figure it out. You'd be Jason Brand. Wore a US Marshal badge? Had some kind of falling out and lost your job.'

'That story is going to stick to me like a burr under a saddle.'

'You still working for the law?'

'Yes he is, Mister Bodie,' Adam spoke up.

'One question,' Bodie said. 'You up here officially?'

'Looking for a couple of fellers. A Deputy US Marshal and a geologist. They went missing.'

'Find 'em?'

Brand nodded. 'The Monks had them as captives. Working a gold find up the mountain a ways. Seems there's a rich vein up there. The Monks have been forcing people to dig for them. By what I heard a few have died doing it.'

Bodie slipped his Colt from his holster and checked it.

'These fellers. They still alive?'

'One of them. Calvin, the geologist, was gunned down while we were on the move from the Monks. Didn't make it. Lawman took a bullet to the shoulder. Had to cut it out. He'll be okay if I can get him down off the mountain and tended to proper. There's a young woman with us. Monks had her captive.'

'Sounds as if you've had a busy time.'

'Could say that.'

Adam had knelt by the stream to splash water on his face.

'Boy seems to take after you,' Bodie said. 'Riding all the way up here to find you.'

'Seems likely. Got a stubborn streak a mile wide.'

Brand crossed to the stream and sluiced water across his own face. He sensed Bodie doing the same.

'I ask you something?'

Bodie turned.

'Depends what it is.'

'I came across a couple of the Monks when I first reached this area. One dead. Other had both knees shot out. That you?'

Bodie nodded. 'They tried to put me down soon as they laid eyes on me. I didn't take too kindly to that notion.'

'I rode up to the house and told them where to find the wounded feller. Next thing I knew they were crowding me and locking me up with Hec Rankin and Calvin.'

'Nice and sociable by the sounds of it. So I'm guessing you didn't stay around.'

'Took the opportunity to refuse their hospitality.'

'So between us we got the whole

Monk clan after our hair.'

'Seems to me you two need to put your heads together over this,' Adam said. 'Taking separate roads all you're going to do is get in each other's way.'

Bodie glanced at Adam, then looked across at Brand.

'Boy has a point. I don't have a problem with it.'

Brand could have argued over the small details. Such as the fact that he had achieved what he came for. He had located the two missing men, so his assignment *was* over. But it went further than that. The Monk clan had shown themselves to be a merciless and troublesome bunch and no matter what, they weren't about to back off and let him go his own way. He couldn't dismiss the known facts. The unruly group were hell-bent on protecting their gold find and they would go to any lengths to achieve it.

They had already killed Joseph Calvin and wounded Rankin. It wouldn't end there if the Monks had their way.

One way or another blood was going to be spilled before the affair was settled. Brand realized getting off the mountain was not going to be easy with the Monk clan on their tails, so two guns were going to be better than one.

He soaked his neckerchief in the stream and ran it over his face. He caught Adam watching him. A swell of pride rose as he caught the boy's gaze. As much as he wanted to be angry he couldn't help but admire the younger man's courage. Riding all the way on his father's trail and facing up to what had happened to him.

Just what you would have done yourself, he had to admit. *A foolish maneuver but what the hell.*

'Looks like we're together on this, Bodie,' he said.

The bounty hunter simply nodded. He crossed to his horse and slid the Winchester from the scabbard, checking it thoroughly.

The man was nothing but professional, Brand thought. He knew Bodie by reputation. The manhunter had few equals. When he went after a wanted man it was a done deal. The Stalker had earned his title and Brand could not fault him. Bounty hunters in general had a raw deal. They were often despised. Looked on as scavengers. Men who hunted and killed for money. But the men they went after were not choir boys. For the most part they were killers. Lowest of the low, and would shoot a man in the back for the dollars in his pocket. Brand had done his share of bounty work. Following his dismissal from the US Marshal ranks he had hired out his gun on a few occasions before signing on with Frank McCord. Even now he was still hunting men and getting paid for it. The only real distinction was he did it with official sanction.

There was a fine line between the two profession and Jason Brand wasn't going to make any judgment where

Bodie was concerned. In the past Bodie, himself, had worn a badge until personal events had turned him away from that life. He had used his learned skills in his new profession and disregarding the way some felt about bounty hunters Bodie had become the best at what he did.

They mounted up and Brand led the way back to where he had left Rankin and Joanne. It took Brand no more than a few minutes to explain about Bodie and Adam. Rankin, still severely weakened, agreed that they needed to move quickly and they made their preparations.

It was Bodie who offered a destination. A town closer than Santa Fe. It had a telegraph facility and more importantly a resident doctor. It offered sanctuary. A place for them to organize themselves and maybe get the help they needed.

19

'Town of Wishbone,' Bodie said. 'West of here. Take us around four, maybe five hours speed we'll be traveling. I met the local law when I came through lookin' for Thad Monk. Name of Dan Conway. He put me on to where I could find the Monk outfit.'

'Has to be the place,' Joanne said. 'Hec needs seeing too fast as possible.'

'That's where we'll head for then,' Brand said. He glanced at Bodie. 'You riding with us then?'

The manhunter took a moment before he spoke. 'Seems likely,' he said. 'Hell, I can't let you tenderfoots go wandering around by yourselves.'

'Thank you, Mr. Bodie,' Joanne said.

'Always willing to help a lady in distress,' Bodie said.

They prepared themselves for the ride ahead. Checked what supplies they had. Made sure all their weapons were fully loaded. By the time they were ready it was full dark.

Brand noticed Adam staying in the background. Saying little. He looked subdued, almost reluctant to be there. Brand crossed to his son.

'Got a job for you, boy,' he said. 'Something needs doing. You up to it?'

'You not feared I'll mess it up?'

Brand failed to hold back a grin. 'Still feeling sorry for yourself?'

'I made a mess of everything. Coming out here. Could have caused more trouble for you.'

'Can't deny that. But you had your reasons. I've been thinking on that. Might have been a foolish move but I can understand why. Promise me you won't don't do anything like that again and we'll let it go. Agreed?' Adam nodded. Brand said, 'When we move out I want you to stay at Joanne's side like a burr under a saddle. She's going to have enough on her hands keeping Hec in place. You be her eyes and ears.

Watch and listen. Keep that rifle close. I'm depending on you.'

'I won't let you down.'

'Never even thought you would. Listen good. Either me or Bodie tells you to do something, do it fast. No questions. Last thing I need to be doing is digging out any more lead from anyone. You hear?'

'I understand, pa.'

'How's the head?

Joanne had tended the gash, cleaning it and wrapping a cloth bandage around Adam's head.

'I'll be fine now the dizziness has gone.'

Brand touched the boy's shoulder. 'No more falling off your horse, boy.'

'Nice family moment,' Bodie said dryly. 'Now let's light out before the Monks show up.'

Brand fashioned a thick blanket pad for Joanne to sit on behind Rankin. Once she was mounted behind the drowsy lawman Brand handed her the reins.

'You going to be all right?'

She smiled down at him. 'We'll be fine.'

'Adam's going to be alongside. He stays with you all the way.'

Joanne glanced at Adam. 'Things are getting better all the time. Now my own good-looking escort.'

'He gets that from me,' Brand said.

Bodie reined in alongside. 'You want me to take the lead? I know the trail to Wishbone from here.'

'Do it,' Brand said. 'I'll ride drag. Watch our back trail.'

* * *

They fell into line, Bodie leading them away from the cluster of buildings and into the shadowed tree line. There was enough light from the stars to at least allow them some guidance across the rough terrain.

They kept sounds down to a minimum, aware that noise would travel far in the mountain stillness. There was little talk. Only the occasional sound from Rankin when a jolt sent pain through his shoulder. With the soft covering of fallen leaves and brush on the ground their passage through the trees was virtually silent.

Brand maintained a silent vigil on their back trail as they moved further and further away from the derelict buildings. Even as time passed and there were no signs of pursuit he still held the feeling they hadn't seen the last of Nathaniel Monk and his kin. Sooner or later they were going to pick up the trail that would lead them to the deserted camp and once that happened they would find the evidence that would show what had happened there. Spilt blood. Soaked rags. It wouldn't take them long to figure out what had happened. And then they would search out the trail left by four horses as they took to the forested slopes and set out for Wishbone.

The Monks knew the mountains and they would figure Wishbone as the closest place where a hurt man could be taken for treatment. Once they were on the trail time would start to run out for Brand and company.

Brand understood the situation. He also understood there was little or no alternative. Santa Fe was too far away. Rankin needed medical help. The choice was made for him. For all of them.

Wishbone offered them relief from their current situation.

Problem was it might also become a trap for them if the Monks showed up. The moment he had that thought Brand corrected himself.

Not if — *when* — the Monks showed up.

Too much had already taken place.

The Monks had suffered casualties. That was something they wouldn't forget. And Brand had engineered the escape of the captives they had been holding. Knowledge of what had been going on went with the escapees and Nathaniel Monk was not the kind to let that happen. He would want to keep the secret of the gold find just that — a secret. From what Brand had learned the Monks would have no problem with carrying out more killing.

When the Monks came they would be on a blood hunt.

Nothing less.

Brand could make out the figure of his son riding just ahead of him. He made a silent promise nothing would happen to the boy. He had just found the boy and determined that nothing — *nobody* — would change that.

* * *

They stopped a couple of times to let Rankin have a break. He was determined not to hold them up but he was still weak and it took both Joanne and Adam to regularly help him to stay upright.

It was well after midnight and into the early hours when Bodie called a final halt. They were on a high ridge that overlooked the wide basin that held the town of Wishbone. Bodie hunched forward, studying the distant, dark township. The place was quiet, with very few lights showing. He was feeling the beginning of an odd suspicion. About things not being as easy as they first seemed.

Bodie always trusted his feelings. In his profession, hunting men who would kill a man as soon as look at him, Bodie had developed keen senses. Inner warnings that made him think long and hard before committing himself to any course of action. He would be the first to hold up his hands and admit to not always going that route. Sometimes he simply went into a situation all guns blazing — often literally — and made the best of it. Right now there was something holding him back. That was warning him to walk soft around Wishbone.

When Brand eased his horse alongside he watched the way Bodie was studying the town below the ridge.

'You figure we've got trouble ahead?'

'What do you see down there?'

'Sleeping town. Nobody moving around. Looks peaceful enough. And that worries you?'

Bodie's slight shrug meant a great deal. 'If I had a middle name most likely it would be suspicious.'

'Suspicious or not,' Joanne said, 'we can't wait much longer. Hec's wound has started to bleed again. He needs that doctor right now.'

Barely above a whisper, Rankin said, 'Don't take risks just for me.'

'Oh, hush,' Joanne said. 'We haven't come all this way for you to die so close to help, Hec Rankin.'

'One way or t'other,' Brand said, 'we need to do something.'

'Seems to me we don't have much of a choice,' Bodie said.

'What if the Monks are waiting for us?' Adam said.

Brand glanced across at him. 'Where did that come from?'

'Well, they know the territory and if

they figure where we've been heading it could be they know a faster way to reach Wishbone. All they have to do is look at our tracks to work it out.'

'Boy has a good notion there,' Rankin managed, his voice even weaker than earlier.

Bodie sighed in frustration. 'Hell, then, there's on'y one way to find out.'

He slid his Winchester free and checked the action.

'If I had a gun I could wave it at them in a threatening manner,' Rankin whispered.

'Enough of that kind of nonsense,' Joanne said. 'You just make sure you stay alive.'

'Yes'm.'

'All this damn talk,' Bodie said, 'is wasting time. 'Fore we know it'll be dawn. We need to reach town before it gets too light.'

'Town's lawman and doctor,' Brand said. 'That's who we need to reach.'

Rankin slumped forward and it took all of Joanne's strength to prevent him slipping from the saddle. Adam leaned across and got his arms around the lawman and between them they helped Rankin stay on the horse.

'Couldn't we stop talking and just do something?' Joanne said.

'Let's go,' Bodie said and eased his horse forward.

They had to make their own trail through the trees and scrub, Bodie choosing the path they rode and his sharp eyes maneuvered them down the undulating slopes. They moved slowly. Not wanting to risk any mishaps as they negotiated the deep shadows. The chill of the night air penetrated their clothing, cold on their exposed skin. Adam slipped off his coat and handed it to Joanne. She made an initial protest, but eventually slipped into the garment. That prompted Bodie to pass over his blanket roll and Joanne draped the cover across Hec Rankin's hunched shoulders.

They traveled steadily over the next few hours, moving ever lower down the angled slopes. The tree line thinned out and they found themselves crossing wide stretches of open ground. The distant town of Wishbone disappeared from sight as they hit deep falls in the land, only to come back into view when they crested higher ground.

Brand fell back a few times, turning to check out the back trail. The darkness made it hard to distinguish anything that might have been out of place. He stayed where he was for some time, checking and rechecking.

Saw nothing.

Heard nothing.

He eased his horse back on the trail, riding easy, but never once allowing his caution to slip away. It only took a moment to miss something, and Brand had the unerring feeling that if any of the Monks spotted them there wasn't going to be any hesitation on their part.

He didn't like the situation. But there wasn't a thing he could about it. It was what it was. He had ridden up into the mountains on assignment, looking for a pair of missing men. He'd found them, under difficult circumstances, and like it or not, he had been forced to take on added responsibility.

The wounded Rankin.

Joanne.

And he wasn't forgetting his son.

Adam had made his own decision to come looking for Brand. Brand hadn't expected him to show up. It had caught him off guard at first. Accepting it had been the only option. All he could now was concentrate his efforts on making sure the boy remained unharmed. Yet even as he thought it Brand knew much of the situation was out of his hands. It only took a single bullet to make a difference. He didn't even want to consider that. Yet it remained in his thoughts. There was no way he could banish it.

Damn and blast.

He needed to concentrate on the current situation. Which was proving difficult.

Bodie called a halt, easing his horse

alongside Brand. Faint streaks of light were starting to dissipate the darkness. Creeping in from the east, the pale luminescence forcing its way across the shadowed landscape.

'Going to be a close one,' Bodie said.

Below them the last distance before they reached Wishbone. The main street stretched away, terminating where it merged with the tracks of the spur line. The railhead was surrounded by cattle pens and corrals. Stables and storage sheds. Wishbone was a gathering place for outlying cattle and horse outfits. The town itself offered the backup for the stockyards. All that was required by ranches and the men who worked for them. It could be a busy place, yet at this early hour it was quiet, deserted, save for lamplight in a few buildings. Smoke rising from chimneys as early fires were started.

'Spur runs all the way to Santa Fe. Wishbone's no more than a cow town but she does good business from what I hear,' Bodie said. He eased in the creaking saddle. 'You set?'

'As I ever will be.'

'Let's do it.'

'Keep on the lookout, people,' Brand said. 'This where it might get busy.'

They put their horses down the final stretch, picking up a well-used trail below that would lead them into town.

20

Bodie led them along the hard baked, rutted street at a steady walk. Fine dust, disturbed by their passing, hung in their wake. He was heading for the doctor's office first. From his previous visit to Wishbone he knew its location. It was halfway along the main street, between a hardware store and a clockmaker's establishment. As they drew rein Brand stepped out of his saddle and mounted the boardwalk. The surgery door was flanked by blacked out windows. A sign on the timber wall to one side of the door proclaimed — *Elliot Kasner, Medical Practitioner*. Brand knocked, waited a reasonable time and knocked again.

Brand and Adam helped the semi-conscious Hec Rankin off the horse, with Joanne monitoring every move. They eased Rankin onto the boardwalk as the unlocking of the door told them the doctor was awake.

The man who opened the door was tall, tending to extreme leanness, his thick dark hair tousled. He stared at them, taking in their general disheveled appearance. Then his gaze settled on Rankin and his blood-soaked shoulder. To his credit the doctor wasted no time on questions.

'Bring him in,' he said. 'Go right through to the surgery in back.'

The doctor closed the door and followed them.

'Bullet wound in his shoulder,' Joanne said. 'He's lost a great deal of blood.'

Between them Bodie and Adam stretched Rankin down on the long leather couch. The doctor immediately worked on removing the stained covering, saying little until he had exposed the wound. He bent over it and examined the raw gash in Rankin's shoulder.

'I'll go find the local law,' Bodie said.

He turned and left.

'What happened here?' Kasner asked, staring at the ragged hole in Rankin's shoulder.

'Took the slug out,' Brand said.

Kasner glanced up at him. 'What with? A broken bottle?'

'We weren't in a position to perform ideal surgery,' Brand pointed out.

'All we had was a knife and a jug of liquor to clean it,' Joanne said sharply. 'It was something that needed to be done quickly.'

Kasner took another look at the wound. 'Have to admit it looks as if you've prevented infection setting in.'

Joanne said, 'Praise indeed, doctor.'

The medic managed a smile at her remark. 'If I caused offense, I apologize.'

'Doc, we've had a long ride down off the mountain,' Brand said. 'We're not at our best right now.'

'Sounds as if you've got problems.'

'Does men with guns following us count as problems?' Joanne said.

'You ever heard of the Monks?' Brand said.

'Some. They live way up high,' Kasner said. 'All I do know is they're not the most hospitable sort.'

Brand pointed at Rankin. 'You got that right.'

Kasner was already rolling up his sleeves and moving to wash his hands. 'Then I need to deal with this man.'

'His name is Rankin,' Brand said. 'Deputy US Marshal.'

'Hec Rankin,' Joanne said. 'You have an assistant, Doctor Kasner?'

'No. Why?'

Joanne stepped to the sink to wash her own hands.

'I think you do now,' Brand said. 'And don't waste your time arguing with her over it.'

He turned to leave, Adam close on his heels.

'Jason,' Joanne said, 'be careful out there. All of you.'

Brand made his way back outside. It was getting brighter. The street was still clear — except for the tall figure of Bodie making his way towards them, with a badge-wearing man close at his side.

'Doc's seeing to Rankin,' Brand said.

Bodie nodded. He jerked a finger at the lawman beside him.

'Dan Conway. Town marshal. I told him what's been happening.'

Conway was in his early forties. A solid-looking man wearing a black suit and a white shirt. He had a wide-brimmed Stetson on his head. His boots looked as if they had been around for some time, though the leather held a shine. Under his jacket he wore a .44–40 Colt Peacemaker with a long barrel in a high riding holster on his right hip. He held out a steady hand to grip Brand's.

'You'd be the Jason Brand used to carry a US Marshal badge?'

'Yeah. Another life,' Brand said. He indicated Adam. 'This my boy. Adam Brand. Right now don't ask. It's complicated.'

'Bodie told me your story,' Conway said. He offered a tight smile. 'If you've crossed paths with Nathaniel Monk and his kin . . . '

'Not the kind to back off easy.'

Conway nodded. 'And Bodie, here, is going after the bounty on Thad Monk. Seems to me you fellers just don't choose the easy life.'

'Choose isn't the word I'd go for,' Bodie said.

Brand said, 'You got a telegraph office?'

'Over at the rail depot. You need to send something?'

'Couple of messages.'

'Give me time to rouse Harry Gilman and get the office open. You and Bodie want to wait in my office. I'll have somebody take your horses over to the livery and look to them.'

'I can stay with Joanne,' Adam said. 'Keep my eyes open.'

'Not so sure about that.'

'Pa, I won't do anything stupid.'

'Make sure you don't,' Brand said.

'And have the doctor look at your head, boy.'

He watched as Adam stepped back inside the doctor's office, closing the door behind him.

'Glad all I got to concern myself with is my horse,' Bodie remarked as he and Brand made their way up the street in the direction of Conway's office.

Wishbone's law office was like a hundred others Brand and Bodie had been in. A room holding a desk and a few chairs. Scuffed and creaking floorboards. Gun rack. Wanted posters pinned to the wall with thumbtacks. A blackened stove already throwing out heat, with an equally blackened coffee pot issuing steam.

'Now that smells damn good,' Bodie said.

A barred door opened onto the cells. To one side was a store room and a small room holding a low cot and clothes chest. Conway's room. The sum total of the lawman's life. Brand knew it well. He had worn badges in a number of towns like Wishbone. The post of local lawman was far from romantic. The pay was small, the hours long, and there was little more to it than that. In most instances a thankless task. Often long on boring routine and sometimes downright dangerous.

Brand stood and surveyed the surroundings in silence.

'Know what you're thinking,' Bodie said. 'Lawman. Manhunter. We both must be missing something in life to put up with it.'

Brand rubbed a hand across his unshaven jaw, wincing when he touched the bruises he'd gained from his set-to with Bodie.

'All the glamor. The excitement. Chances to travel and meet new people. Get shot at. What's not to like, Bodie?'

Bodie leaned against Conway's paper-strewn desk.

'You got me there.'

There were tin mugs hanging from hooks on the wall near the stove. Brand took a couple and poured coffee, handing one to Bodie. They were sampling the coffee when the door opened and Conway came in.

Bodie raised his mug. 'We helped ourselves.'

Conway took a mug and filled it. 'Telegraph office will be open for business by the time you walk over.'

'Obliged,' Brand said.

Conway took his seat behind the desk. He leaned back in the creaking swivel chair. Threw his hat on the desk and studied Brand.

'I have to ask,' he said. 'You say the boy with you is your son?'

Brand sensed Bodie showing interest. He might have known who Adam was but it hadn't gone further than that yet. Brand told his story. Simply and brought the pair up to date.

'And you never . . . ' Conway said.

Brand shook his head. 'Met him on the train when I was leaving Washington. Didn't know he existed until then.'

'Must have been a hell of a surprise.'

Bodie choked off a low chuckle. 'Not

as much as if it had been a girl.'

The thought had never occurred to Brand until that moment.

'Hell, you're right about that.' He drained his mug. 'I'd better get over and send those telegrams. Bodie, you want to check on the patient.'

Conway said, 'I'll take a stroll through town. Folk will be starting to move around any time now.'

He reached for the gun rack and took down a 10-gauge Greener shotgun with cut-down barrels. He hung a small canvas bag holding extra shells around his neck.

They went their separate ways, Brand making his way up to the end of the street and through the business section, passing the cattle pens and corrals. The pens were empty. One of the corrals held a number of horses and a man was forking hay into the feeding troughs for them. He barely acknowledged as Brand walked by. He skirted one of the store huts and saw the telegraph office sited on the rail platform. As he walked closer the side door opened and a skinny, middle-aged man rushed out. When he saw Brand he waved his arms, signaling in alarm.

'You the feller Marshal Conway said was comin'?'

Something told Brand he wasn't about to receive good news.

'What's wrong?'

'*Wrong?* I'll tell you what's wrong,' the man said. His voice was high with agitation. 'There ain't no telegrams going out, that's what's wrong.'

Brand stepped up close. '*Why?*'

'Because the line's dead,' Harry Gilman said. 'It was fine when I closed up last night. Now there ain't a peep out of it. Not a goddamn peep. You know what I think, mister, I think somebody went and cut the wire. Can't see any other reason. Been no bad weather. Nothing to cause damage.'

Brand stepped back, scanning the area, searching for any movement that shouldn't have been. He raised the Winchester, feeling a jolt of concern.

If the telegraph wire had been cut, isolating Wishbone, it was more than likely the Monks were behind it. And if that was so it meant they were around.

Here in town.

In Wishbone.

'I'll send out a repair crew,' Gilman said. 'Could take a while.

And then Brand heard the abrupt whip crack of a rifle firing. More shots followed.

Brand spun on his heel, ignoring Harry Gilman's questions.

Damnit, he thought. *They're here in town.*

Close on that he felt a cold fist clutch at his chest.

Adam.

At that moment nothing else mattered.

If they had hurt his son . . .

He dug in his heels and took off at a dead run. Heading back towards the main street, and hoping he was not too late . . .

21

It turned out to be a day to remember. When the town of Wishbone experienced its one and only, genuine gunfight, and as with most confrontations of its kind it was short, though decidedly not sweet. As the retelling had it and the facts were embellished, the legend grew each time it was related — yet even if it had been reported strictly it would have been enough . . .

★ ★ ★

. . . Brand found himself moving down the center of the street, eyes seeking movement in the alleys between buildings. He had slowed to a walk, wanting to be in control if he had to shoot.

He sensed a shadow of movement as Bodie stepped into view from the doctor's office. One of the office's windows had been shot out. Across from Bodie a figure lay sprawled in the street, a bloody patch staining the back of his shirt. A ragged exit wound. The manhunter saw the expression on Brand's face.

'He wouldn't back off,' Bodie said. 'Nobody hurt inside.'

Conway stepped into view. He approached them.

Bodie had been checking out the rooftops. He caught a glimpse of a dark figure showing himself above the false front of the saloon. Early sunlight gleamed on the barrel of a rifle.

'Roof of the saloon behind you,' he said. 'Rifleman.'

Brand turned, caught a glimpse of the hiding man.

'I see him,' Brand said. 'Let him show himself . . . '

'You any good with that?' Conway asked.

Brand didn't say a word. He waited until the man moved to get a better shot. As soon as he did Brand brought the Winchester up in a smooth motion, held, squeezed the trigger. The crack of the 44–40 broke the silence. The distant figure slipped sideways, then flopped forward to hang over the edge of the saloon roof. His rifle dropped from his hands and spun to the street below.

'Guess that answers my question,' Conway said.

A figure burst into view from where he had been concealed behind crates and barrels stacked outside a dry goods store. He held a massive .44 caliber Walker Colt in his left hand, the muzzle belching thick black smoke as he triggered a shot. The sleeve of Conway's jacket flapped as the ball passed through it. Wishbone's lawman turned at the waist, the Greener recoiling as he fired. The shot caught the shooter in the stomach, shredding clothing and flesh. The force of the shot shoved the man back, bouncing him off the solid wall of barrels and crates. He went down hard in a welter of bloody flesh, kicking away the remainder of his life on the sun-bleached boardwalk.

'Damn,' Conway said, 'nothing I hate worse than a sneaky backshooter.'

'Talking about backshooters,' Bodie said. 'There's *my* man.'

He had seen more armed figures moving out from the cover of the big livery barn next to the cattle pens. He made out seven of them. All armed.

Led by Nathaniel Monk.

Bodie's attention was drawn to the broad shouldered, scar-faced figure of the man he had come searching for.

Thad Monk himself.

'He's mine,' Bodie said.

'You got to catch him first,' Brand said.

'Yeah? Well watch and learn, pilgrim. Watch and learn.'

* * *

'Listen to me,' Nathaniel Monk called, his voice deep and loud on the quiet street. 'Give me the girl and the lawman and we'll leave peaceable like.'

'Too late,' Brand said. 'They already told us about your damn mine. Killing them won't change that. The telling is out now. You need to put down your weapons and surrender.'

'The hell you say. Damn you, there needs to be a reckoning. A price to pay for those of our kin you bastards killed and wounded.'

'I had a feeling he was going to reason things like that,' Conway said. He was thumbing a fresh load into the Greener as he spoke. 'There goes a quiet day in town.'

The first shot came from one of the Monk rifles. Fired in haste and well off target. The slug kicked up a spume of dust to one side of Bodie's advance. He maintained his course, ignoring the opening shot, and breaking off to the left. His rifle snapped to his shoulder and he aimed briefly, but with enough accuracy to place his shot into the shoulder of the errant shooter. The impact pushed the man off balance and a second shot from Bodie hit him in the chest, kicking him backwards.

Brand picked up a tall, lean figure raising a worn, 1873 *Trapdoor* Springfield carbine. He didn't hesitate. He brought the Winchester round and let go a shot from the 44–40, levering the next round into the breech before the first brass casing hit the ground. The distant figure let out a coarse grunt as the lead slugs hammered his chest. He fell back, finger jerking on the carbine's trigger, sending the 45–70 caliber shot skywards.

Brand watched as the Monks retreated. Backing to the cover of the barn. They hadn't been expecting such fierce opposition. He saw them pull into the shadows of the building while they considered their next move. There was one certainty — the Monks would not be quitting anytime soon.

'Keep them pinned,' Brand said.

Brand skirted the corral. The man who had been forking out feed had already taken himself away from the scene. Brand pushed himself hard, angling around the rear corner of the barn and reaching the rear doors. He could hear the muffled sound of voices. The crackle of gunfire. Bodie was keeping the Monks well occupied.

Flat against the wide doors Brand used the end of the Winchester's barrel to ease open a way in. The doors swung slowly apart.

Brand hoped his luck would hold long enough to let him get inside. That might have happened if one of the doors hadn't issued a loud squeal of dry hinges.

'Somebody comin' through the back door,' a man yelled.

'Go deal with it, Turk,' a deep voice ordered.

As the door swung wide, letting light fall across the straw littered floor inside, Brand saw a dark figure detach from the group at the front of the stable. A rifle snapped out a shot. Brand heard the thud as the slug hit the door on his left. In the brief moment before he moved he saw a bulky figure pounding in his direction, the man muttering as he triggered more hasty shots at Brand's shape framed in the patch of light from the open door.

Even with all the noise Brand heard Turk's rifle click on an empty breech. The man kept coming, stepping into light as he closed on the rear of the livery. Heavy-shouldered, with a thick, dark beard, he laid a hand on the revolver tucked in his belt.

'I remember you from the house,' he said. 'We had you locked up with those other two.'

'Then you'll know I don't give in easy. I'd advise *you* to quit now. Before I put you down.'

The look in Turk's eyes as he stared at the leveled rifle in Brand's hand revealed his thoughts. He *wanted* to draw and fire. The need was strong. He licked at his lower lip, savoring the taste, and the hunger in him was so clear. His face was shiny with sweat.

'You killed them,' he said. 'They were kin. Can't forget that.'

'They pushed it,' Brand said. 'You've all been pushing. Couldn't let it lay. They made their choices ... same choice you have.'

'*Damn your eyes, you murderin' sonofabitch.*'

'Right now,' Brand said, 'I can see it in *your* eyes. You figure to take me? Go ahead because I won't walk away and show my back. Way I heard it that's the way you Monks prefer to do business.'

It was one jibe too far.

Turk uttered a wild, savage scream and went for his gun.

It was barely halfway drawn when Brand shot him.

Turk dropped to his knees, face registering the shock from the 44–40 slug that had burned its way into his body. He made another attempt at pulling his gun, so Brand put a second slug into him. The lead pellet struck directly over Turk's heart and he toppled onto his back.

'It's over,' Brand called out, taking cover behind a wooden stall. 'You're covered front and back. Give up.'

Nathaniel Monk's powerful voice yelled back.

'I'd sooner die than surrender . . . '

Brand sighed.

This, he thought, *is going to end messily*.

22

'I want that sonofbitch bounty man,' Thad Monk said.

'Damn you, Thad,' Nathaniel Monk said. 'You walk out there that man will put you down like the mad dog you are.'

'I ain't afeared of him. You think I got a yellow streak down my back?'

'Seems I have to wonder about that. I never raised no son to shoot a woman in the back. Can't pretend that didn't happen, boy.'

'I brung you money from that bank.' Thad scowled. 'Shootin' that woman was an accident . . . '

'So you say but it's brought trouble to our door and family have died with that bounty man showing up. We was doin' fine enough diggin' out that gold.'

'Ain't right that Bodie sonofabitch

trailin' me. I aim to make him pay for that.'

'Lord help me, boy, I got sons back home all shot up because you brought trouble on us.'

Thad jerked his handgun from the holster, muttering to himself as he thumbed in fresh loads. He had a second revolver pushed behind his belt and fresh loaded that.

'Now step out of my way, old man, I got killing to do. Rightly don't know why I waste my time listening to you. You figure I'm scared? Damn your eyes, I'll let you see me kill me a bounty man, and then we can settle this.'

Thad glanced at the two surviving Monks flanking his father.

'You want to do something? Go see who shot Turk down. I got better things to do.'

He stepped up and kicked the barn door open.

'*Got the guts, bounty man?* Tired of you doggin' me all over creation. Face to face, you bastard.'

233

He burst out through the swinging open barn door, a gun in each hand, hammers back and muzzles rising . . .

* * *

. . . the exchange had taken seconds, giving Brand the time to move along the barn floor, catching the action at the far end as Thad Monk pushed open the doors and stepped through.

He saw the shadowed pair of figures move away from the barn door, coming in his direction and he raised the Winchester.

A gunshot blasted. Flame and smoke.

Brand stepped forward, dropping to a low crouch, reducing his bulk. A second shot sounded. He felt the slug kick up dirt inches away. He tripped the rifle's trigger, levered and fired again. Kept firing until the rifle clicked on empty.

One of the advancing figures lurched sideways, a low cry forming in his throat as he caught a pair of 44–40 lead slugs. The second man ran forward, punching out shots that went wide. He darted to the side, flattening against the barn wall.

Brand dropped the empty rifle, snatched the Colt from his holster and extended his arm, snapping back the hammer. Took a breath and forced himself to remain still as he settled his aim on the fast-shooting man. He felt a keen burn as a slug razored his right cheek. Felt hot blood stream down his face. Clenched his jaw and sighted along the Colt. Eased back on the trigger. The Colt bucked, a lance of flame issuing from the muzzle. The heavy slug hit the poised figure and knocked him back, his weapon suddenly off line. Brand rose to his full height, Colt steady in his hand as he fired again, and again, the slugs slamming into the jerking figure. Through soft flesh, impacting against rib bones and shattering them. The man hung against the barn wall, mouth open long enough for a drawn-out sigh of expended air to escape, then slumped down and lay still . . .

* * *

. . . Bodie saw the stocky figure move out from the barn, a revolver in each hand.

Thad Monk.

The man he had climbed the mountain after.

'I'm taking you in, Monk,' Bodie said. 'And they're going to hang you.'

'Like hell,' Thad yelled. 'Ain't no back shooting bounty man besting me.'

'You got that wrong. Back shooting's your style . . . not mine.'

Bodie saw the muzzles of Thad's pistols start to rise as he screamed a mouthful of obscenities. They were cut off when Bodie's rifle fired, sending a volley of shots that cut Thad's legs from under him. Bloody gouts erupted from Thad's limbs as he crashed to the street. His pistols thundered and sent slugs into the ground. Thad twisted in

236

agony, letting go of his guns and clutching at his shattered legs.

The powerful figure of Nathaniel Monk burst from the barn, his pistol firing as he showed himself, anger distorting his face.

The second shot he fired burned a line across Bodie's right side.

His hammer was going back for a third shot.

The Greener in Ben Conway's hands boomed. The searing blast of shot caught Monk in the high chest, tearing a bloody hole. The impact threw him backwards. He hit the barn door, rebounding and falling face down in the dirt. He rolled onto his back and lay staring up into the dawn sky, one side of his face a mask of sprayed blood.

And as quickly as it had started the gunfight was over.

Brand walked out of the barn. He glanced at the bodies on the ground. Put away his gun and crossed to where Bodie stood, noticing the spreading blood patch on the man's shirt.

'That hurt?'

Bodie inclined his head as he stared at the wound.

'Like hell,' he said. He glanced around at the hesitant figures of Wishbone townsfolk emerging from doorways. 'You think the rest of the day will turn out quieter?'

'Don't want to appear inhospitable,' Conway said, 'but I hope you two don't make a habit of visiting Wishbone too often.'

Brand touched his fingers to the bullet burn on his cheek.

'Amen to that,' he said.

Over Conway's shoulder he saw Adam walking down the street in their direction. He moved out to intercept his son.

'You're hurt,' Adam said, staring at the blood on Brand's face and shirt.

'Looks worse than it is.'

'Is this what happens every time you ride out?'

'Comes with the job, Adam. It's what I do.'

'You ever figure that's the problem?'

Brand couldn't argue with that.

'How's Rankin?'

'Doc says he'll pull through. He's stitching up the wound right now. Says it's going to take some time for Hec to recover. Joanne's saying she's going to stay in town with him.'

'That figures. I think that young woman has taken a shine to Rankin.'

'At least one good thing came out of this then.'

Brand managed a weary smile. 'More'n one I'd say.'

'Doc in this town is going to be making a profit,' Bodie said as he walked by.

'Adam, go see the telegraph man. Find out when he'll have the line repaired.'

'All right, Pa.'

As Adam made his way along the street Conway said, 'That look on your face tells me you ain't got used to him calling you that yet.'

'I might never get used to it,' Brand said, but if he was truthful it was already starting to become familiar.

23

The telegraph manager turned out to be well organized. He sent out a repair crew to search for the break in the line. They located it a few miles out of town and set to repairing it. By midday the work was completed and the telegrapher was able to transmit Brand's messages. He sent one to McCord, a second to the US Marshal's office in Santa Fe. He also sent a third message — to New York. By the time replies came in Brand and Bodie were emerging from Wishbone's hotel after baths, shaves, and climbing into the new clothes purchased from the handiest dry goods store. Adam was wearing a fresh set of clothing and a clean bandage over the wound in his head.

McCord's telegraph response had been brief, to the point, and despite a degree of reluctance, he agreed to the leave of absence Brand requested. He added a line telling Brand not to be away for too long. The US Marshal office advised that a team would be sent to Wishbone to follow up on the matter of the Monks and their involvement in the death of Joseph Calvin and the wounding of Hec Rankin. An investigation would be launched into the suspected kidnappings and deaths of the forced mine workers.

It had been a busy time in town. Conway had arranged for the local undertaker to deal with the dead. Doctor Kasner tended to Thad Monk's leg wounds before he was locked up in the jail, filled with enough morphine to dull the pain. Bodie would transport him to stand trial when Kasner pronounced him fit to travel.

Bodie called in at the jail where Conway was dealing with an increased paper load. He found Brand already there.

'You fellers have made me a lot of

work,' Conway said.

'Comes with the job,' Brand said. 'I'm trying not to think of the reports I'll have to fill out when I get back to Washington.'

Bodie smiled. 'I ain't got a single form to fill in. That reminds me, Conway, you got my reward claim filled out?'

'First thing I did.'

Conway found it and handed it over. Bodie folded it and put it away.

Leaving the marshal to his paper-work Brand and Bodie made their way to Doc Kasner's surgery and climbed the stairs to the upper floor where a couple of rooms were fitted out for recuperating patients. They found Rankin, his shoulder heavily bandaged, being tended by Joanne. He was propped up on pillows, still pale and weak.

'I owe you my life,' he said. 'Damned if I don't.'

'No bad language,' Joanne chided him, though there was a smile on her face. 'And I don't want you two tiring him.'

There was a firm tone to her words that told Brand and Bodie who was in charge.

'We won't be staying,' Bodie said.

'Marshal's office is sending a team out to look into the Monk affair,' Brand said.

'If they need any information,' Joanne said, 'I can help.'

'Well I'm sure they will appreciate that.'

'I got things to tell them too,' Rankin said.

'We both have,' Joanne said, her eyes fixed on the lawman.

Brand couldn't fail to notice the way the young woman made no attempt to hide her feelings for Rankin, or the way he responded to her ministrations.

'Rest up,' Bodie said. 'We'll leave you to it.'

'Leaving Wishbone any time soon?' Rankin asked.

'Take a day or two to sort things out,' Brand said.

As they left the room Joanne followed them, closing the door behind her.

'I never really got a chance to say thank you for what you did. But I will now. To both of you. I won't forget what you did.'

'You just look after Hec,' Brand told her. 'He's a lucky man. Keep him safe.'

Joanne colored up, but nodded. 'Oh, I intend to do just that.'

She turned and went back into the room.

Bodie stared at the close door. 'Almost had me in tears there,' he said. 'You think they'll ask us to the wedding?'

'You're a hard man, Bodie.'

'It's all show. Hope the next time we cross trails it's a sight more peaceable.'

'Have to say it's been interesting,' Brand said.

★　★　★

Two days later Brand and Adam were ready to leave Wishbone. The US Marshals had arrived in town, conducted their business and moved on to investigate the Monks. Bodie was preparing to escort his prisoner for trial, and Brand was eager to move on.

He shook hands with Bodie.

'Boy, you heed what your pa tells you,' Bodie said to Adam. 'Sometimes he talks a deal of sense. *Sometimes.*'

After Brand and Adam had left the jail Bodie sat across the desk from Conway.

'You got any fresh wanted flyers in amongst all that paperwork?' he asked, figuring it was a good time to look to what he was going to do once he had handed over his prisoner and collected his reward. He saw no reason not to check things out while he had the chance. Never knew what might be on offer.

★ ★ ★

Brand and Adam rode the spur line all the way to Santa Fe where he had business to tie up before they caught the mainline train that would start them on their way to the east coast, New York, and a meeting with someone who, Brand hoped, could provide him with a solution to something that was heavy on his mind.

Brand hadn't seen Virginia Maitland for some time. He knew she was still busily involved in restoring her company to its former level following the attempt to take it from her by the man who had been her legal advisor. It had been that affair, culminating in the frantic pursuit through the snowy Montana mountains, that had brought Brand and Virginia together. Their feelings, developed during that violent time, had grown stronger and it was only the nature of their ongoing business that kept them temporarily apart.

Now, Brand wanted to see her. Tell her about Adam, and hope she would be willing to help. The boy deserved a better chance at life than Brand could offer. He was going to ask Virginia if she could give his son that opportunity. He understood she might be reluctant to take on Adam, and he would understand if she said no. Yet despite his misgivings Brand had to make the attempt. He owed it to his son. He owed it to Lisa, Adam's dead mother. They had parted on less than good terms and Brand had never had contact with her from that day. She had made it clear she didn't approve of his drift towards a violent existence. He hadn't understood at the time. Now he did. It might be too late for him. He was set in his life. But Adam was young enough to be steered away from it. As much as it might hurt Brand had to try. To guide his son along a clearer path.

It might not fully clear his conscience — but he had to at least make the attempt.

We do hope that you have enjoyed reading this large print book.

Did you know that all of our titles are available for purchase?

We publish a wide range of high quality large print books including:
Romances, Mysteries, Classics
General Fiction
Non Fiction and Westerns

Special interest titles available in large print are:
The Little Oxford Dictionary
Music Book, Song Book
Hymn Book, Service Book

Also available from us courtesy of Oxford University Press:
Young Readers' Dictionary
(large print edition)
Young Readers' Thesaurus
(large print edition)

For further information or a free brochure, please contact us at:
Ulverscroft Large Print Books Ltd.,
The Green, Bradgate Road, Anstey,
Leicester, LE7 7FU, England.
Tel: (00 44) **0116 236 4325**
Fax: (00 44) **0116 234 0205**

SHOOTOUT IN
CANYON DIABLO

Steve Hayes

Canyon Diablo offers Lute Latimore
a fresh start . . . provided he can live
long enough to enjoy it! The plan is
simple — go to work as a deputy for
his brother Heck, the town marshal.
But Canyon Diablo is a hell town,
with a reputation for chewing up
lawmen, and Lute becomes a target
as soon as he pins on the star. One
night, a fusillade of bullets changes
everything, and suddenly a new trail
beckons Lute — a killing trail . . .

GARRETT'S TRAIL
TO JUSTICE

Terrell L. Bowers

Dayton Garrett is a roving trouble-shooter, taking on jobs from town-taming to bringing down a counterfeiting ring. Charged with searching for a missing child, he fetches up in Shilo, where his attorney brother Knute provides him with helpful information — and requests a favour in return. Alyson Walsh has been convicted of murder in a kangaroo court, and faces the noose in two days' time. Knute wants her broken out of jail while he endeavours to get her a fair trial — and Dayton is just the man for the job . . .